THORNWOOD ACADEMY 1:
NEVER SAY DIE

LJ SWALLOW

I am terrified
of this dark thing
that sleeps inside me.

Sylvia Plath

Chapter One

"Sweetest girl, I've asked you more times than I can count —please do not attempt necromancy without your mother present."

I frown at my father's words. "I thought biology class would be more interesting if the dissected animals fought back."

He rests against the edge of the mahogany desk in his study, hands in dark jeans pockets, expensive blue shirt stretching across his toned chest, every bit the deceptively charming man he is. The lecture continues, but I barely listen to a word as I stand before him. I'm secretly smug that my plan worked—the human high school didn't appreciate my attempt to brighten the boring day and I'm not welcome back.

I'd say I'm one of two people who dare ignore my father Dorian Blackwood, head honcho on the supernatural governing council. The only other person is my mother Eloise, who sits in the nearby brown leather armchair, ever elegant, even in her black leggings and loose emerald green sweater.

Dorian Blackwood and Eloise Thornbrook, beautiful and deadly, vampire-witch hybrids nobody dare cross. Upset Dorian and you'll lose your life—like countless victims from his past killing sprees.

"I haven't reanimated any humans, what's the issue?" I continue.

Eloise leans forward and attempts to take my hand between hers, so I hold them behind my back. "Violet. Sweetheart. If you refuse to fit in at a human school, then you'll need to attend Thornwood Academy."

No. I've avoided the place for the whole of my eighteen years. "I'm not going there. Every supe knows who I am—my parents named the academy after themselves. I've a reputation before I even set a foot in the place."

My mother's eyes fill with disappointment at my tone. I resemble her more than my blond-haired father—we've the same long, dark hair and pretty features, but my personality is ninety percent my dark and deadly father's. My mother's ten percent keeps the world safe from Violet Blackwood. Mostly.

Thanks to Dorian's desire to foster better relations between human governments and his own supernatural one, I'm the victim of a diplomatic attempt to integrate his daughter into a human school. Some would argue that the other students were victims, but I haven't hurt many. No deaths, anyway.

"I've always wanted you to attend Thornwood, Violet. I know you'd thrive," she continues.

"Thrive?" I snort. "Like a weed growing in a dung heap?"

Dorian pulls himself from the desk and lifts my chin, smiling down at me. He's charmed *so* many people in his life with that smile and the stunning blue eyes I inherited. "What's wrong with weeds?" he asks. "They're harder to kill than pretty flowers."

"Because they strangle the life from everything around them?"

"Violet," Eloise puts in sharply then looks to Dorian. "Many in the supernatural governing body are eager for our child to attend Thornwood. I've always argued that Violet's… temperament doesn't fit the human schools you shochorn her into, Dorian. We've had too many incidents with Violet misusing her magic abilities. Human schools can't help her *discipline* those talents. Thornwood can."

"Ah, yes. Like mother, like daughter." Dorian chuckles and then winces as Eloise spikes magic into his mind. I can't help smirking at her action—exactly how *I* shut people up.

"The time I used necromancy was a mistake. I never intended to use the spell to reanimate my grandmother," she retorts. "Violet's was—"

"Practiced from a young age?" I suggest.

Eloise stands, and suddenly the pair of them are looking down at me. Uh oh.

"Your decision to reanimate mice isn't the only issue, Violet," says Eloise. "There was the incident with Katy and that poor boy."

"She asked for my help," I retort.

"I don't think Katy wanted you to daub runes on the wall with his blood," Eloise says and throws Dorian a look when he snorts a laugh. "A simple hexing spell would've sufficed."

"Katy told me she wanted to tear Archie's dick off for cheating on her," I say. "You should be proud that I recognized she wasn't serious and didn't remove any appendages."

I struggle to recognize when people aren't speaking literally, a side-effect of avoiding the world my whole life. So, *I'm* proud that even though I believed Katy's request was serious, I considered the situation carefully and chose a less permanent injury.

3

The whole incident genuinely confused me. Why ask a powerful supe to help and then freak out when she uses a spell?

"Human girls are so emotional," I mutter.

Dorian continues to fight a smile. "As are human guys when you shrink their dicks." Eloise elbows him and frowns when I snicker too. He gives her an apologetic look. "Sorry, sweetest, but you have to agree that's inventive and a *little* amusing. I hope a guy never upsets you, Violet."

"I won't hesitate on the dick removal if anybody approaches me with an unwanted one."

Again, Dorian chuckles. Sighing, Eloise reaches across his desk and takes hold of a pamphlet then taps it in the palm of her hand. "You're attending Thornwood," she replies tersely. "Dorian and I have discussed this and made the decision."

"*What?*" I choke out. "No. No supernatural schools. Those kids are more painful than humans. Can't we go back to homeschooling?"

"No. After a parade of terrified tutors, your reputation means that nobody else wants the role. You're also too detached from the world. You need to become part of that now that you're older, Violet," Eloise continues and passes the pamphlet to Dorian. "You're powerful but dangerous."

"You mean, too much like my father?" I arch a brow. "And like you, mother?"

"Exactly," says Eloise.

I brighten a moment. *The answer.* "And Zeke and Ethan? Do they agree to this?" I can usually rely on my other two fathers to side with me, especially against Dorian.

"Yes. They have agreed." Eloise smiles.

But not side against my mother. My teeth grind. "I won't stay at the academy. I'll leave."

"Oh, yes you will stay, sweetest girl," replies Dorian.

"Otherwise, I'll remove your access to the library and take back your grimoires. No more studying our rarer spells."

My jaw drops. "That's blackmail."

"That's doing as your parents tell you," he replies.

"Like you did?" I bite back.

Dorian's expression darkens and Eloise shakes her head at me, eyes wide. He stands and the anger that rarely appears these days seeps out, invisible but consuming the air around. His tone switches, the wrong button pushed.

"I *could* behave like them if you wish, Violet. Lock you up and force you to do my will. Turn you into a weapon against your own kind. How do you think *that* would end?"

"As badly as it did for your parents?" I suggest and meet his challenging stare. "Tell me again how you burned them alive."

For a horrible moment, I think he's about to raise a hand to me, but Dorian does something once alien to him. A skill he's managed to learn over the last few years.

He takes slow calming breaths.

"Watch your tongue, Violet," says Eloise cautiously. "That was a cruel thing to say. You can be a heartless, thoughtless girl sometimes."

"Thank you, I've been working on that." I flash her a smile then snatch the pamphlet from where Dorian crushes it in his hand. "The academy wouldn't let me attend, anyway. As you say, I have a reputation."

Dorian pushes his tongue against a sharp canine and leans closer. "They will. I *had* arranged for you to start next semester but after that little performance, I've changed my mind. You're moving to the academy next week." I glower as he pats my cheek. "It's about time you learned a lesson or two."

I'm stunned and wishing I'd kept my mouth shut as he stalks from the room, and I wince when the walls shake as he slams the door. Eloise takes my face in her soft hands and looks down at me. "You worry me. You're too much like your father, Violet."

"And that's a problem, why?"

What behavior do they expect from the daughter of Dorian Blackwood and Eloise Thornbrook, two of only three immortal vampire-witch hybrids in the world? I'm the third since my dumb parents never considered contraception might be needed in the throes of their ridiculous passion.

They never made that mistake again. One baby Blackwood hybrid is more than the world needs.

A father with sociopathic tendencies, and a mother who can wield all schools of magic, some illegal? I'm the perfect darkling child. My parents can send their daughter where they like, but I'm not staying.

Chapter Two

Thornwood Academy.

Oh, joy.

Once, the supernatural schools were named Nightworld academies with no humans attending. Since the Confederacy and Dominion crumbled, and Dorian's regime began, the years of vampires, witches, and shifters hiding—at times ineffectively—ended. Human and supernatural worlds became one. I'd say 'one big happy family' but perhaps 'relatives who tolerate each other for the holidays' is more accurate.

Hence, leaders of this brave new world created new academies that humans also attend in order to work towards a peaceful future.

There *was* another supernatural academy back in the day —a reform academy on a Scottish island. Dorian tore down the place once he ended the old Confederacy government, after exposing their crimes against the students.

Dorian met my mother at Ravenhold academy—a heart-warming story of hybrid boy meets witch girl and both want to kill each other. Obviously, neither tried hard enough because, for an unfathomable reason, the beautiful young things fell in love. The pair had a mutual desire to kill other people, so I guess they found something in common.

Nobody speaks about Ravenhold now, but I imagine it looked a little like the academy I'm staring at. Why did the supes choose to establish their schools in falling-apart, gothic buildings? They could've built something more like a modern high school and at least pretended that supes want to adopt human ways.

As always, Dorian and Eloise turn heads the moment they step inside the gray-bricked, imposing building. The pair are mesmerizingly beautiful with a raw power that emanates from them, sensed by all races. I've always hidden in their shadows, even though people I meet enthuse at how pretty I am too. The same people who wander away whispering how much I'm like my parents in 'other ways'.

But there's worse than head-turning. Girls gawk at Dorian and whisper how 'hot' he is. *Gross.* He might look like a 'hot guy' but he's *middle-aged* not the twenty-something he appears to be. Immortality equals 'hot' forever, and of course he loves the attention. I sometimes wonder if he were the Dorian Gray from the old book, what would his portrait look like?

Only when my parents leave me with the two head teachers, am I aware I can't hide in my parents shadow any longer. The human guy in his brown suit reminds me of the uptight, gray-haired principle who kicked me out of the last school. Only this guy's dark-brown hair is as bushy as his beard and matching thick arm hair pokes from beneath his white shirtsleeves.

The black-haired woman... at first I think she's a blood-drinking, hemia vampire, but she's forcing calm into the atmosphere. That's a trick that the energy-feeding pneuma vamps use, but also a school of magic practiced by mind-altering witches. Either way, the skill will help her with discipline.

I'd guess vamp–she's younger looking like my parents, with the same flawless skin and telltale facial bone structure all vampires share—cheekbones you could cut yourself on.

A human and a supe jointly overseeing the academy? How delightfully tactful.

Mrs. Lorcan still seems flustered by her famous guest even though he left minutes ago, whereas Mr. Willis frowns as he leafs through a thick black book, muttering about using 'a bloody computer' instead.

"Where do we put her?" he asks in a Scottish accent, flicking faster. "She's not allowed a single room because she's *his* daughter."

Thanks, Dad, you could've at least insisted on *that*. I've never shared anything in my life.

"Rather tricky," says Mrs. Lorcan in a soft tone. "Violet doesn't fit into either the witch or vampire houses. I hope that doesn't cause issues."

"Well, your students can be 'rather tricky'." He slams the book closed. "Are you more vampire than witch, Blackwood?"

"Are you more human than ape?" The man can't even address me by my first name. Rude.

His jaw clenches.

"That's the answer." Mrs. Lorcan stands and straightens her powder-blue suit jacket sleeves. "Violet can live with the humans."

I laugh to myself at her joke until I realize this is *not* a joke. "I'd rather not. Humans never understand my idiosyncrasies. Most don't even understand what the word means."

"The humans who attend Thornwood are intelligent, Violet," she replies.

"And unfortunate." I tip my head. "How can this mix

work? The hemia vamps are on the cusp of becoming full-time blood drinkers, and the influence of rampant hormones on the lamia vamps could be 'distracting'."

She gapes but it's true—lamia vamps feed on sexual energy once they're mature enough. The academy's older kids are most definitely mature enough.

"As for the witches..." I wave a hand. "Cliquey, I imagine. Usually, they're arrogant assholes who judge each other based on a family's place in our society. Humans are way beneath them."

"We *make* this work," says Mr. Willis. "Thornwood students are our future leaders, and the races must learn to co-exist. Your society only revealed yourselves fifteen years ago. The students here are the first generation for the new world."

"Mmm-hmm."

"And that is why our new student must live with humans," insists the headmistress. "Why not ask your son to accompany Violet to the house building, Mr. Willis?"

With a huff, the headmaster takes his cellphone and texts a message. A reply pings almost immediately. Blowing air into my cheeks, I gaze at the pictures on the wall to avoid more conversation. Three student houses, each standing or sitting in rows like the human classes in high school photos, but with one difference.

Every student looks the same from this distance.

"You have a *uniform*?" I ask in horror.

"We're all equal here, Violet, and this is one way to reinforce that equality." The headmistress smiles. "You may wear your... normal clothes in the evenings and on weekends, or if you visit the local town."

"Normal clothes." The headmaster shakes his head.

"Is my clothing an issue?" I ask. "I find black suits most occasions." Black. *All* black. Leggings. Long skirt. Lace-trimmed shirt. All accessorized with one silver teardrop pendant on a chain necklace that holds a secret. Simple yet effective, as are the heavy boots if somebody upsets me and needs a quick reminder how fast my reflexes are. "Saves time looking for clothing to match."

"Nobody can see your eyes behind all that black."

"My black extends beyond my eyes, Mr. Willis. I'm sure you've heard stories."

The oak door behind swings open without a knock to alert us, and a guy my age stands in the doorway. I'm immediately drawn to the uniform I distantly saw on the pictures—at least the pants are black but the blazer...

Yellow stripes.

Yellow, with a matching tie.

The guy flicks a look the length of me and then frowns at his father. "That's not human."

"Perceptive," I reply and look at the headmistress. "You're correct, the human students are intelligent."

"Then why are you joining Darwin House?" He continues to look at me as if I'm something unpleasant stuck to his shiny black shoe.

"Not through choice. Don't worry, I'm not staying long."

"This is Violet. Violet—Wesley." We study each other to reach our snap judgements. Popular kid who excels at sports? He's big. Broad shouldered, square jaw, buzz cut hair. If I had a type, this guy wouldn't be it.

Something in his expression tells me the feeling's mutual.

"You're enrolled permanently," says the headmistress. "Wesley. Please accompany Violet. She can share with Holly."

"Oh? Is that a different way of grouping students? Those with botanical names?" I ask. "Interesting."

Nobody responds to my wit, and I turn on my heel. "Let's get this over with, Wesley."

I sense I haven't made the best first impression on Wesley

as he silently walks through the tall-ceilinged hallway, past the white-washed brickwork interspersed with arched windows and doors. Other uniformed students pass by, and stare at Wesley more than me.

He marches me back out the doors I entered with my parents and leads me through an archway set in a wall that borders a courtyard. A path leads to a smaller building, detached from the main academy, but still gray bricked and delightfully depressing beneath the gloom that I hope is perpetual. I don't burn in the sun, but I don't like it.

The moment we pass behind the wall, thick fingers grab my upper arm and yank me to one side.

"We don't like vamps in Darwin House," says Wesley in an attempt at a menacing voice.

"I'm not a vamp."

"Or witches."

"Nope. Try again."

His expression becomes poisonous. "They let another *shifter* into Thornwood? What does a little Goth girl turn into? A raven?"

"Nevermore." I smile.

"What?"

"Never mind."

His fingers bite harder. "Don't fucking mess with me."

"Then I suggest you remove your hand from me, otherwise there will be a mess when *I* remove it from *you*."

He sneers. "If you're not a supe, I'm not scared of you, little girl."

I wrench my arm away and cross them both over my chest. "I am not a little girl or a 'Goth'. Although I'm perhaps a little dead inside since I'm a vampire-witch hybrid and I enjoy necromancy."

He stares at me. "Bullshit. Who are you? Violet what?"

"Violet Blackwood." The surname registers and he tenses.

"And yes, I'm exactly like my father. Just less with the throat-ripping. For now."

I bare my teeth, holding my ground as he closes the space between us, squares his shoulders, and looks down.

"I don't often get physical with girls to keep them in line, but I can make an exception. You need to get the fuck out of Darwin House and away from Thornwood. You're not welcome."

Smiling, I reach up and pat his cheek. "Now *that*, I agree with. We've found something in common already. How lovely. Do you think we'll be good friends?"

Stepping by, I walk ahead towards the building he was leading me to. Humans still keep themselves separate, it seems.

Chapter Three

GOOD GRIEF.

This girl can't be human.

"Are you sure you're not a shifter?" I ask Holly as she bounds along the hallway with me trailing behind. "A Golden Retriever?"

"No. Shifters don't attend Thornwood." She's practically *bouncing*, her auburn curls flying around her face.

I wonder what would happen if I threw a ball?

Wesley dumped me in a common room that I made a mental note to avoid in the future, and then he walked away muttering. Suddenly, I came sullen-face to freckle-face with a slender human girl who'd look as if she walked out of my last school if it weren't for the awful uniform. Since we met, she hasn't stopped talking.

"Oh!" She stops abruptly and I almost knock into her. "What do you eat?"

"Eat?"

Her voice lowers to a whisper. "I heard that Dorian Blackwood eats children."

"Yes. But I can never eat a whole one and father claims that's wasteful. I stick to eating steak."

Holly's jaw almost slams into the floor.

"Holly, I do not eat children and neither does my father. What a ridiculous question," I sigh. "Do continue."

"Yes!" *Did she just clap her hands in glee?* "Our room!"

Taking a steeling breath, I follow her into a room that perversely smells of violets. I'd pictured two beds uncomfortably close in order to foster friendship, and zero personal space. Instead, there's enough room to not hear Holly breathing at night.

There's also space for Holly's plethora of cushions on the floor and for me to skulk opposite, safe from conversation. This is helped by her room divider printed with orange cats.

I'd feared a communal bathroom to accommodate *every* female student, but our room has one. Small mercies.

I walk to the window and peer down at the small lawn below. "Good. This is high enough to throw someone out of should they annoy me."

She gawks at me for a moment then gives a little laugh, expecting me to smile at my joke.

I don't smile.

Often.

"Right. Um. Allie left a couple of weeks ago; I'm glad to have a new roommate."

"Why?"

She blinks. "Company. I tidied your space since I'd spread my things across the room." Holly points to an impressive pile of belongings on her bed. Wow. The girls at high school had lockers overflowing with all manner of pointless objects; Holly has a roomful.

"I see," I say, and glance around *her* space. The shelves at the side of Holly's bed are stacked with framed photos of many, many people. And ceramic pigs. A *lot* of ceramic pigs, in all imaginable sizes and colors.

"Do you collect those?" I ask and point.

Holly digs into the pile on her bed and pulls out two plush pink pigs, one tattier than the other. "Kind of."

"There's 'kind of' a lot of porcine paraphernalia." She looks at me blankly. "Pigs."

"As a kid, my grandmother would buy them for me every year, and after a few years everybody thought I collected them. Now I do." She grins and hugs the pigs. "Do you collect anything?"

"Souls."

"Pardon?" The pig's face squashes out of shape in her grip.

This girl... "That was a joke."

"You're very hard to understand, Violet. And a little intimidating. Excuse me if I don't know whether to believe you or not."

"I collect books. Old books." Grimoires. "Is Thornwood's library large?"

"Maybe?"

"You can take me there," I inform her.

"Don't you want the school tour first? Meet some other students?" Her mouth turns down when I choke on my own saliva. "I know *everybody*."

"I imagine you do. You're very... amiable."

"Thanks." She grins. "Not even a little tour before we reach the library?"

Closing my eyes, I push my tongue against my top teeth. "Fine."

By the time I've opened them, she's already out of the door. This Golden Retriever energy is going to exhaust me.

I LOSE FOCUS ON HOLLY'S BABBLING RUN DOWN OF THE school's social hierarchy within minutes. The academy halls are nothing like the human high school—no notices advertising inane activities that establish dominance in the social hierarchy, nor graffiti sneakily scrawled around the place. No lockers to loiter around. Not that I loitered by or used mine.

Somewhere between ground zero (or, as Holly calls it, the cafeteria) and the classrooms, a girl accosts us. Everybody I've met is in uniform and the pale girl with long, dark hair wears a yellow chiffon scarf artfully tied around her neck. An attempt to add her own flare?

There's no magic or vamp aura around her, but there is one of superiority over Holly. Holly introduces her to me as Isabella, Darwin House's head girl, and we exchange tight smiles and greetings. Isabella asks questions about an end of semester dance and my brain protests, so I stop listening.

Pursing my lips, I gaze around at the kids flowing through the building. Looking at the size of some, I'd say those I've met so far are the eldest in an academy that's more populated than I expected.

Good. Plenty of chances to hide amongst the masses.

Across the hallway, a guy sits on a bench beside a classroom door. Or more correctly, sits on the top of the wooden bench's back with his booted feet on the seat. He watches me in a way that'd freak out some people, and I deliberately stare back.

With a smirk, he hops down and saunters over. The guy wears his hair tied from his face, midnight brown and shoulder length. His vampire features are easily recognizable —hemia always have the same perfect faces designed to seduce. His dazzling green eyes no doubt aid him with potential conquests.

He's built like a lot of vamps our age too—not a bulky

man, but definitely not as slender as a boy. Apparently, something he wants everybody to know since his black shirt and jeans emphasize his honed body. He's cultivated quite the image with his unnecessary-indoors leather jacket. No uniform for him—*such* a rebel.

"Hey, Grayson," says Holly, but he doesn't even register her presence.

He looks me over. "Are you the Blackwood girl?"

"And are you the academy's misunderstood loner?" I reply.

"Pot. Kettle."

"I'm not misunderstood. I'm always crystal clear about how I feel. Or don't feel." He looks at me expectantly. "Yes. I'm Violet Blackwood."

"Grayson Petrescu." He jerks his chin. "I heard Dorian's kid was joining us."

"Petrescu." I slant my head. Interesting. "Related to the deceased Oskar Petrescu?"

"Distantly," he says, his expression darkening.

"Ah. Let me guess, you act out because you hate your family name. Having corrupt relatives would do that to a boy." I tap my lips. "And a fanboy of my father? I can't imagine why else you're so eager to introduce yourself."

"I have relatives who helped your father," he retorts.

"And a relative who locked my parents in a corrupt reform academy."

"I don't know what you're talking about, but I don't like this vibe between you," interrupts Holly, gesturing at us.

"Vibe?" Grayson scoffs. "You spend too much time with the witches and their pretty crystals." He steps back and there's no sign of the awe any longer. "And I am *not* a fanboy."

His tall figure stalks away, without the swagger this time,

and Isabella laughs. "Catch you at lunch," she says and wanders off.

"You won't make friends if you behave like that," says Holly, tone serious.

"Precisely. And *your* friend? What interrupted this scintillating tour?"

"I'm on the committee who organizes the Spring Ball."

"My condolences."

She pouts. Actually *pouts*. "You have to come. The dance is the *best* night of the year."

"I'm not masochistic enough to subject myself to teen mating rituals." Holly stares. "I don't like social occasions," I say in simpler terms. "Dances. Parties."

"Trips to the mall?"

"Are you insane?" I reply. "I don't like people and certainly don't want to mingle with them while they fill their meaningless lives buying things they don't need."

Holly huffs. "Your negativity is tiring."

"As is your endless enthusiasm."

"Do you ever smile?" she continues. "Or is the miserable face all part of your act?"

"Act? Oh, Holly, the only acting I do is pretending to be interested in Thornwood and your tour."

Holly blinks rapidly and then presses her lips together. "You're rude and arrogant, Violet Blackwood. I'll excuse your behavior today because you're new and obviously stressed, but I hope you change your attitude."

Human girls. What do I say now? "Thank you." Holly turns away, and I add quietly, "I do like that you understand me already."

Chapter Four

HOLLY CAUTIOUSLY DEPOSITS me at the library with the promise she'll return in an hour and take me for something to eat. I protest that I'm not ready for the cafeteria and she informs me her friends eat lunch outside, and that means I have no excuse.

How wonderful.

The library was the one place I liked at the human high school. Mostly because hardly any students used the place, and those who did weren't the boring ones who tried to taunt me. Plus, the librarian didn't care if I borrowed more books than permitted. I think she was just glad to see someone.

This library will be different. History books. Spell books. Parts of the old world hidden from me.

Rows of desks with dividers are located between shelves, and my spirits lift as I walk to the back of the library, following the old book smell like a moth to a flame. Abandoned pens and books that students couldn't be bothered to re-shelve cover the scratched desks towards the front of the library, but back here the desks are clear.

Thick books cram between thinner ones on these shelves,

some with embossed gold words on the spines and others not marked at all. I run a finger along them like a child in a candy store, sensing if any hold magic the way my mother taught me. I'm not skilled in picking up energy and history by touching objects like some witches, but I'm more attuned to books than people.

My mother Eloise is a Trinity witch—one of few skilled in all magic schools, including necromancy, and I've inherited many of these skills. *Was* a witch. I'd presumed she was created as a hybrid the way Dorian was until one day I discovered she died, and Dorian turned her as she took her last breath. *How romantic.*

Dorian's mother is the one who killed Eloise, which could explain why I don't have much interaction with my grandparents.

That, and because my father killed them both, for Eloise and in revenge for a childhood I'm not supposed to ask about.

One of my favorite skills that Eloise passed on to me can't be used around books—I enjoy fire and can manipulate flames. This innate ability wasn't well-controlled at first, but she taught me not to burn everything. I once had a fire serpent familiar, but I didn't pay him enough attention, so he singed my fingers and left me.

That caused trouble because familiars aren't supposed to leave their witch. He was never well-behaved and there were a few unexplained fires in the area soon after; I expect he's still out there happily indulging in arson.

I pause on a thick book that holds stronger magic than anything else in here and pull the burgundy leather-bound tome from between the others. This isn't marked as a grimoire, but witches once hid magic encrypted inside non-spell books. The Blackwoods notoriously shared underground magic this way—well, the Blackwood witches who created

Dorian and handed him to the vampires. He's Blackwood by name only.

As I flick open the cover, somebody snatches the book from my hands. Pissed, I turn to face the thief. A guy stands close to me and now has the book clutched against his chest. Witch. I sense his magic immediately. A *powerful* witch.

Steel blue eyes meet mine as I scowl at the guy. He's in the academy uniform but looks as if somebody dragged him through a bush, his messed-up brown hair and unbuttoned jacket setting him apart from the smartly dressed clones I've met.

"This belongs to me," he says. His accent is familiar—the cultured English found amongst the higher class witch families.

The ones who believe they're superior.

"It's a library book," I retort. "Therefore, it belongs to nobody but the academy."

Ignoring me, he drags another from the shelf and thrusts it at me. "Here."

I return the black book to its place and point at his. "I'd like to read that one."

"No."

"And your continued possessiveness of that book intrigues me." I hold a hand out.

He snorts. "I'm a Willowbrook and this library was founded by my grandfather. Therefore, the books are mine if I want them."

"I'm a Blackwood and my father oversees the council who founded the new academies. Therefore, the books are mine if I want."

Momentarily, his eyes widen, and he peers at me. "Blackwood? When did you arrive?"

"Today. But I'm leaving soon."

"Tonight?"

"No. My parents are headed to Europe on vacation. Or for Dorian to depose another dictator and take the role himself. I'm never sure which." The guy blinks. "Then, I'll use my blood runes and return home."

"Blood runes?" He scoffs. "They're on the list of magic that's forbidden inside the academy."

"Oh good. That might aid me in getting expelled." What is with this guy and his precious book? "What type of witch are you?" I ask.

"Elemental."

"Which element?"

"All."

"Impressive. What's in the book?"

He snorts again at my swerving the conversation. "Words."

"In any particular order?"

"What's your name?"

"Violet. Are they spells?" I reach out again and he steps back.

"I'm Rowan."

"I don't care. What's in the book?"

A smile creeps across his face. "Pages."

"You're ridiculous," I retort. "And annoying."

"Mmm." His irritating grin grows. "Like meets like."

"I'm nothing like you." I retort.

"Of course not. Because you're *special*." He picks up a bag he dropped on the floor beside the shelves and shoves the book inside.

"Who my parents are makes no difference to my position here." Is he seriously about to steal that book?

"No." He taps the side of his head. "*Special*. I hear you're deranged and practice necromancy."

"Yes. Necromancy has its place."

I've never met anybody who bothered talking to me for

long—if you discount Holly and her talking *at* me, and I do not have the inclination or energy to deal with Rowan.

And he has some really *weird* energy about him, which is saying something if I think so.

"Well, enjoy your stay at Thornwood." Rowan focuses on fastening his black rucksack.

"Thanks, I won't. Where's your room?"

"I don't entertain guests, especially not one who wants to take my things." He looks up. "Unless I've made such an impression that you want to visit for other reasons?"

"Ugh." I wrinkle my nose. "Certainly not."

"Well, don't follow me." Rowan hitches the bag onto a shoulder. "Although, I'm sure we'll become acquainted soon, Violet Blackwood. It's inevitable."

Before I can respond, Rowan moves along the space between the shelves and ducks back into the main part of the library.

Violet Blackwood.

Few know that my original name was Mia, and that as a toddler I accidentally renamed myself. One day, my parents introduced me to some distinguished guests as Mia, and I protested that my name was Violet. They corrected me; I had a tantrum. This happened with other guests too, and after the third time, I exploded into a fiery rage. I was *not* Mia. After dealing with the smoldering rugs, my parents discovered the answer.

I'd frequently heard, "The Blackwood's daughter is violent." Except I'd *mis*heard this as Violet.

Dorian found the mistake hilarious and promised he'd call me Violet from then on. My mother reluctantly agreed since we were still at the 'teaching Violet not to burn the house down' stage and a name change was better than moving homes.

My other fathers, Zeke and Ethan never knew the reason why. They were just surprised I chose such a pretty name.

Sometimes, I wish I'd stuck with Mia because I am in no way a flowery or colorful girl. I did once die my hair violet but currently prefer a midnight blue that's almost black. And violent? Less so, these days.

Today, I consider whether that might change despite my parents spending years teaching me not to connect with my emotions. This way, I learned to control any extreme responses to others upsetting me.

Dorian didn't need to worry. Since the name change incident, I can't remember ever feeling strongly about anything past mild irritation.

Let's hope that doesn't change.

Poking at the hole where the book should belong, I huff. I didn't want to use my magic against anybody while I'm here but so far I've met three people who changed my mind.

Whether he's aware or not, Rowan has thrown down a challenge. I *will* get that book.

Chapter Five

As I wait for Holly, I'm still irritated about Rowan and his book. If he'd waited until I finished reading, I never would've noticed how precious the thing is to him. Therefore, I wouldn't be interested.

Or would I have read something Rowan didn't want me to and become *extremely* interested?

I've lived in a world of secrets my whole life, with the truth drip fed to me over the years. Perhaps that's one reason why my parents kept me away from society until I'd grown magically strong enough to control myself.

Holly returns to find me flicking through books that contain nothing but dubious history that paints witches as heroes. I'd considered leaving before she arrived and not accompanying her to wherever these kids eat, but I'd like to see who Rowan hangs out with.

I'm disappointed to discover he isn't there.

The groups sitting in the square between the main building and the two attached wings *are* similar to the human school, although here small cliques revolve around the school houses rather than the kids' level of aptitude in physical or intellectual pursuits. Personally, I find dividing the races into houses creates unneeded rivalry and segregation, but I suppose there's a reason.

Did the academy once try to mix them up? Perhaps the results weren't favorable. I do spot witches with vamps, but the humans sit separately on the lawns, guarded from their supernatural peers. Including my new friend, Wesley.

"Right!" Holly straightens and scans the grounds around us, waving and mouthing 'hey' to a few of them.

"Don't introduce me," I say sharply, and keep my position beneath a large oak tree's canopy.

I struggle to read people, but I've identified that Holly has two expressions: confusion and exuberance. "Why?" she asks.

"I don't want forced introductions. People should have the choice whether to communicate with me." She opens her mouth in protest. "False smiles and disinterested hellos whilst making snap judgements based on my appearance? No."

"Does that mean you won't sit with *my* friends," she retorts, and her out of character tone catches my attention.

She *is* a source of information I'd rather not lose. "As you've been nice to me and if this desperately matters to you, okay."

I reluctantly leave my shelter beneath the tree and follow Holly through the groups to where her human friends sit in the early spring sunshine. Someone told me it rained all the time in this part of the country, and I'm not happy—they lied. There's no gray cloud in sight.

Does Holly see what I mean about the hellos and fake smiles? I forget every name as soon as I'm introduced by Holly, although I do recognize Isabella and her artful scarf. I remain standing, annoyed when Holly tugs at my sleeve and I'm forced to sit on the ground.

None seem particularly interested in who I am, so there's that.

Holly passes me one of the sandwich wraps she brought with her and pulls two bottles of water from her bag.

"Thanks," I say as I cautiously unwrap the paper, peering at the filling. "Chicken?"

"Not your usual diet?" I look at Wesley as he speaks. *Not this again.*

"No." I take a savage bite and chew as our eyes remain locked on each other.

"Violet doesn't eat children," puts in Holly, silencing not only our group but the witches beside us. "That's a rumor."

I raise my eyes skyward and swallow the mouthful. "Well, thank you for that unnecessary clarification, Holly. My mother is gluten intolerant and so we rarely eat bread at home."

I swear the silence thickens and a girl beside me snickers. "A gluten intolerant vampire. How is that even possible? There's no gluten in blood."

"Holly, could you please enlighten your friends *what* my parents are. Not now. Later." I examine the wrap. "This tastes good, thank you."

She stares. "Was that *gratitude?*"

"I do have some social skills; I reserve them for special occasions."

"You're fucking weird," says Wesley.

"Thank you."

"That wasn't a compliment."

"But it was. Or do you want me to pretend that I care about your opinion?"

Those around tense. Ah. The alpha of their little human pack. Wesley mutters something beneath his breath and turns away.

"Do you share classes with the other races?" I ask the nondescript girl beside me.

"We attend graded classes, the same as we'd study at a normal school," she replies. "Some supes attend too. Their classes don't apply to humans—we don't have magic, nor do we need help in controlling our *primitive* side."

A girl who'd I'd struggle to tell apart from Isabella points at a guy. He's standing in front of three girls who're seated on the only bench in the area. I can't see all three of them clearly, because he's a large guy, but one girl looks like a lamia vamp to me, especially considering how he's transfixed on her pretty face.

In fact, the guy stands before them as if he's having an audience.

Interesting.

"Leif is a shifter," she explains. "His family wanted him to attend Thornwood."

"But there's no house for shifters," I say. "They don't attend academies anymore."

"Half-shifter," puts in Holly.

Hybrid shifter? "Half what else? Is he a mid?"

How much silence can I inflict on this group because I appear skilled at it.

"Don't mention mids," says Holly. "He's half-shifter because his mother's human and wants him to get a diploma. Most shifters don't attend school at all."

"Why not mention mids? They're as much part of society as you are nowadays. My other father is one."

Shifters who transform into their animal forms before they're old enough get 'stuck' and aren't popular in shifter society. Some mids look more human than others, depending on how much they keep their animal's features. This animalistic mix up also alters their behavior and not in a good way.

Ethan, my moodiest of fathers, is a dragon mid. He's closer to human than dragon, save for his eyes and a few scales, but does have the mid-like tendency to lose his temper violently. Again, something happened years ago that my family won't discuss.

As if my status as Dorian's daughter isn't bad enough, this newly revealed connection sets me higher up the weird scale.

"Humans don't trust them. *Mids* still kill," says the girl who pointed.

"*Still kill* and don't cover their tracks, you mean," says Wesley tersely.

"Are you implying that the other races kill on occasion? And that this is unacceptable?" I ask.

"Uh. Yeah," says Wesley.

"Then add your race to the list of indiscriminate killers. That doesn't set us apart from you."

"We're not *encouraged*," says the nondescript girl. "I bet you are."

I regard her but don't deign to respond.

"Let's just eat lunch," interrupts Holly.

Okay. I can't resist. "Quite the opposite. I'm a necromancer."

This time the silence is interrupted by Isabella choking on her apple.

"So don't worry. If somebody dies, I can assist." Yet more silence. "I *am* joking."

"I know. Nobody can perform necromancy," says Wesley derisively.

"You misunderstand me." I unscrew the water bottle lid and drink deeply. "I'm joking when I say I'll assist. I don't need anymore pets."

"You bring people back to life and keep them as pets?" asks Isabella in a familiarly horrified voice.

I shrug and stand. "Sometimes I make them do tricks, does that count?"

This time, I don't tell them that I'm joking.

After all, a girl likes a little mystique.

And I'm still mad that my parents took my pets away.

Chapter Six

AFTER ANOTHER SPELL in the library to clear my head, and unsure whether my new, over-exuberant friend will be in our room or socializing, I take a walk around the academy. I consider whether to use some elemental magic to give the place a rain-drenched, stormy atmosphere, but frankly I can't be bothered. I'm better spending my time planning how to leave. My parents are overseas; they wouldn't notice at first.

And if there's no way out, I'll work on getting expelled. I have some skill in that.

I'm walking through the cloisters towards the path leading to the human house building and hear loud voices. Laughter. Shouting. Males taking part in a bonding session. With a sigh, I continue my walk in their direction. If this is Wesley, using magic and getting expelled could come sooner than I hoped.

Someone snatches my arm and drags me away from the covered walkway into a shadowed nook. The idiot doesn't consider my reaction and magic pulses from me, knocking my assailant to the ground.

A guy.

Stomping across the pavers in my thick-soled boots, I

32

prepare to challenge him further, but he's on his feet in seconds and partially blurs as he moves further away from the walkway around the cloisters.

Vampire.

Well, I share your speed, my dear friend. I dart in the same direction, then halt in front of a wall blocking my way. Crap. He's behind me in a heartbeat but sensibly pauses before touching.

"I suggest you *don't* touch me," I say softly and slowly turn.

Grayson, his mouth set in a thin line, his eyes shining a brighter emerald in the dark. He's swapped his leather jacket for a hoodie which he has drawn over his face. Either the guy favors the same clothing color as I do, or he's dressed to blend in.

"Keep your voice down; I'm helping you," he says.

"I needed assistance with what? Visiting this wall?" I purse my lips. "Stand aside or I'll hit you again. Magically."

"I said, keep your voice down," he snaps.

As I open my mouth to retort, he pushes me back into the shadows, but yelps when I seize and twist his wrist. The nearby voices drop away for a moment. "Violet. The humans are hunting," he says, voice low.

"Hunting?"

"Yeah. Wes and his little minions get drunk most nights and scout the campus for stray supes." He drags his wrist from my hand. "The luckiest end the night with only a few bruises. The unluckiest… much more."

Stepping back, I look him up and down. He's less bulky than Wesley and his friends, but vampires hide a preternatural strength in their lean physiques. "The supes don't fight back?"

"No, *they* get the blame if the human assholes get hurt because the headmaster is the bastard's father. Wesley gets away with everything." Grayson's eyes blacken—this is one annoyed vamp.

"And you think these dumb humans would attack *me*?" I ask derisively. "Your act of bravery in order to save the dark maiden from her foes is unwarranted and unwanted. I'll deal with them." The vampire takes my arm again as I try to turn away. "Grayson. Let me go."

"You'd land in deep crap if you hurt one of them."

I look over my shoulder and smirk. "Bad enough to get expelled? Perfect."

"Fine. You do you," he says with a scoff.

Confusion washes over me as Grayson releases my arm and disappears, reappearing the few meters away at the edge of our hidden spot.

"Hey, assholes," he shouts.

Footsteps thunder and Grayson's figure disappears a second time as two large males barrel into him.

What is the insane vampire doing?

Shouting and laughter ensue, and I walk to the edge until I can see but remain unseen myself. Three guys wearing hoods pulled far down across their faces attempt to pin Grayson to the ground. A third jeers at him—Wesley, also hooded. Huh. A vamp that can't fight off drunk humans?

There's another yell, this time not triumphant. The two guys who'd almost-held Grayson down now lie several meters away, one on the ground by the low wall, holding his head, the other on his front groaning.

And Wesley?

Held by the throat, lifted from the ground, feet dangling uselessly. His hood has fallen from his face and wide eyes gleam with fear. "I'd do everybody a favor if I got rid of you," Grayson snarls. His lips are drawn back, mouth split into a vicious smile, shaper teeth glinting.

"Is that a threat?" chokes out Wesley.

"Touch me or any of my friends again and you'll find

out." That raspy tone is familiar—a pissed vamp on the verge of attack.

"You have no friends." One of the other guys staggers to his feet, spitting blood onto the pavers.

Still holding Wesley by the neck, Grayson turns. "Don't I? Because I know some others who'd fucking love to take down a pathetic human bully. Or three."

When nobody replies, Grayson sets Wesley back onto his feet and pats his cheek. "Run along now."

Wesley rubs at his neck, then squares up to Grayson. "I'll have bruises from your *sudden, vicious ambush*, asshole."

"I don't give a shit."

"You will tomorrow." Wesley jerks his head at his friends, both now standing but keeping a sensible distance. They stride away, heads high as if *they're* the winners. Perhaps they are. As the pack passes through the archway out of the cloisters, I prepare to leave.

"You can come out now," says Grayson. "They won't hurt you."

I'm about to retort I don't need his valorous help when instead he walks away from me, towards another part of the cloisters. I shrink back again as Grayson emerges from the dim area with a slender girl.

Huh?

Grayson doesn't hug or touch her, and they walk at a distance from each other as he accompanies her to the main academy building. She's stammering her thanks and shaking as she passes me, and I blink as I watch him leave with the short-haired witch. Grayson doesn't so much as glance in my direction.

How curious. Do we have a vampire vigilante here?

I dig hands into my heavy coat pockets and move to sit on a bench in the middle of the cloisters square. If I immediately make my way to Darwin house when the guys are still around, that'll lead to a tedious exchange.

Stretching out my legs, I tip my head up, wishing for rain.

Or a thunderbolt to slice through Wesley and his guys.

I don't give a crap that Wesley hates and would like to attack me. In fact, I'd find the situation amusing. But I'm as much my mother as my father, and she hates injustice.

Small-dicked males picking on others, including females? Unjust.

I'll ensure his humiliation occurs in front of a large crowd. Before Grayson carries out his threat.

Chapter Seven

I'M unsure what's worse—the tightness of the white shirt collar and yellow tie or the blazer. Refusing to wear *everything* that I'm told, I slide on my Docs rather than the prescribed shiny shoes. I spent the night reading a book I borrowed from the library, fascinated by how violent human history is too, and slept in. An effervescent Holly woke me, and I explained I'd rather not eat breakfast with the humans. Holly solemnly understood and promised to return with something because I 'can't go all morning without eating anything'.

Am I her new project? The poor lost girl she's taken under her wing? Amusing. People are usually only nice to me if there's something they want from my father or the council—the human kids barely bothered with me at high school, apart from Katy. She dressed the same as me and saw me as a kindred spirit. No. Unlike me, the silly girl has her sights set on a romance with a vampire.

We had a mostly silent friendship, and Katy never questioned my state. The only thing she asked of me was to make her ex sorry for the way he treated her.

Which didn't end well for anybody involved.

But Holly? She couldn't be more *unlike* me.

As I finish dressing, the mirror mocks my conformity, and I scowl back.

No.

I'm not doing this. Last night was the final straw—I've no desire to be part of a turf war between students, and I certainly won't be seen in public wearing *this*.

I've resisted using blood runes up until now, but illegal or not, I'm casting a spell today. The academy rummaged through my luggage when I arrived and found a small, enchanted dagger, which they confiscated. At the time, I mumbled a false apology and resisted curling my hand around the pendant I wear.

Pulling off the tie I'd struggled to fasten, I take that long silver pendant from around my neck and slide it apart.

The half-inch thin spike glints and I frown at the blood stain before carefully rubbing the metal with a finger. A sharp object doesn't need to be knife-length to do the trick. This works.

Blood magic is in my... blood. Blackwood magic blood runes interfere with the ether and offer a convenient means of travel, but only if you've visited the place you aim for at least once in the past. With my parents in Europe, home won't be an issue.

I first attempted blood magic as a toddler, which horrified my parents once they realized I wasn't having accidents with stray knives lying around the kitchen. My early attempts didn't work; I've inherited vampire healing, otherwise I'd be covered in scars. My quick healing isn't as powerful as a vampire's, nor is my magic pool as deep as a witch's. Annoyingly, I'm partially weakened by the hybrid split, but still stronger than most overall.

Choosing a spot close to my bed, I kneel. As I slit my finger and draw runes I memorized years ago, I can smell my own. Thicker and darker than human blood, there's a peculiar tang different to the faint scent I get from other races' blood.

I'm partial to blood, but only my own to use in spells; I've never tasted any other. If I stop using the potion I've taken daily my whole life, that could change. My mother created the concoction, which dulls my ability to scent blood and rids me of the desire to consume any. Tastes like strawberries.

Dorian and Eloise don't take blood from anyone apart from each other, and in situations I don't want to picture. That blood lust—or any kind of lust—would interfere with my desire to remain disconnected. That's another reason emotions are messy: the physical activity this leads to. Why would anybody want to mix their secretions with another's?

Ugh.

I'm still completing the intricate rune, ensuring the lines intersect perfectly, when a shriek echoes around our tall ceilinged room. Holly stands in the doorway, face wan as she looks at my bleeding hand.

"Violet! What's happening? Did someone hurt you?" She dashes over and stops dead as her eyes switch from my bloodied fingers to my handiwork. "Omigod! What's *this*?"

"I'm drawing a rune," I say and gesture at the unfinished symbol. "A spell to leave the academy."

"In *blood*?" Her hand goes to her chest, but her eyes remain wide. "If you'd asked, I would've fetched you some chalk. That's what Amber uses."

"Useless. I need to use my blood for *this* spell."

"Blood magic is illegal, Violet. Don't get into trouble on your first day." Holly kneels beside me and attempts to take my hands but stops herself when she looks at the blood.

"There is no first day. I'm leaving." I hold up the spike to cut a second finger. "Let me finish in peace. This won't hurt you."

"No!" Holly snatches the chain from my hands then shrieks. Again. She flings the thing to one side and stares at her palm.

Good grief. I sigh. "Did you cut yourself on the pendant?" Eyes welling, Holly presses fingers into her other palm as she nods. "That's a side effect from grabbing sharp objects."

The girl now stares between me and the blood seeping from the deep cut, eyes flicking a look at the rune as her face grows paler. Perspiration beads on her forehead and Holly's face becomes whiter than a starved hemia vamp.

"Holly. Are you okay—?"

Obviously not, since she slumps forward, unconscious, face knocking against my chest.

Fantastic. I peel Holly from me and set her down so she's lying on the rug, then lick my fingers to stem the bleeding with my handy vampire saliva. The academy put me in a room with someone who can't stand the sight of blood?

Ha ha, that someone has an odd sense of humor.

Leaning over, I take her sliced palm and grimace. The blood doesn't tempt me at least, so nothing changed there. But I'm not licking *her* hand. Instead, I moisten my fingertips and press them against the wound to stem the bleeding.

Holly's eyes snap open at my touch and, in momentary confusion, she screams at me before blinking. "Oh," she croaks.

"Why are you screaming?" I snap.

"I opened my eyes to a vamp in my face," she mumbles.

"I am not in your face," I retort. "Why did you pass out?"

"I faint if I see blood." She groans and turns onto her side, then stretches an arm out, pointing across the floor. "I brought you a muffin, but dropped it."

I sit back on my heels. "*That's* what you're thinking about right now?"

"I panicked. I thought someone had hurt you."

"I don't mind the sting. Look at–" Holly interrupts me with a retching sound. "Please don't vomit."

"*Omigod*!" I'd forgotten how much human girls screech. A girl—Jo?—from yesterday's uncomfortable lunch situation steadies herself on the doorframe and looks between us, gaping.

"What are you doing?" she shrieks again. "Holly! I knew this wasn't safe."

"What *are* you talking about?" I ask and stand as Holly struggles to sit.

"Vampires shouldn't room with anybody but their own kind." Jo's voice wavers as her gaze travels between us, fixating on the bleeding. Then she sees the rune. "What are you doing to her?"

"Nothing," croaks Holly and steadies herself with a shaking hand. "I'm fine. I fainted."

"You're bleeding!"

And how I'd also forgotten the human capacity to overreact.

My gloomy morning grows darker as Wesley appears beside Jo. "That's because Violet used magic on Holly's mind."

"I did not!" I stand.

He shoves into the room, and I'm suddenly engulfed by his presence and his overpowering cologne. "You charmed Holly and then took her blood. Is that why you weren't at breakfast? Waiting for a different meal?"

I choke out a laugh. "I don't drink blood. And if I were going to attack anybody, I wouldn't choose somewhere I'd get caught."

"*When*, not if," he replies, and I grimace as I wipe his spittle from my face. "I'm taking you to my father. He'll want to know about the Blackwood's attack on a human. You need removing from the academy."

A tiny ray of sunshine. "You think I'll get expelled for attacking another student?"

"That's at the headteachers' discretion."

"She didn't attack me," protests Holly.

Wesley turns to pull Holly to her feet. "Don't worry. We'll find the truth. She'll get what she deserves."

There's an impressive group of people in the doorway now, including Leif, his height setting him above all those in front of him. He watches impassively, brown curls falling across his forehead. Once I meet his eyes, he arches a brow at me, then walks away.

Chapter Eight

I GIVE Wesley a little wave as he reluctantly leaves me with the headteachers' secretary, who instructs me to step into a room adjacent to hers and wait for their summons.

She stares at the blood on my hands, and I bare my teeth to demonstrate they're as clean as when I brushed them this morning. Tutting, she waves me through the door again.

I step into a wood-paneled room with two uncomfortable-looking black leather sofas arranged in an L-shape. At the high school, I spent time waiting in a similar room several times. That one had noticeboards pinned with various suggestions on how to get help, and illegal activities to avoid. This one? Nothing.

Only Grayson sitting on one of the sofas looking oddly non-descript now he's in uniform. Apart from his eyes. Unusual color. Only when he doesn't look away from my staring into his eyes do I realize he's trying to hold my gaze—and there's a hint of a smirk.

Hmm. I look away and flop onto the other sofa.

"What did you do?" he asks curiously.

I look back to him. "Cut myself."

"Huh? The nurses' room is at the other end of the hallway."

"I'm no longer bleeding. Neither is Holly."

Grayson takes a sharp breath. "Did you attack her? I mean, Holly's annoying, but there're better ways to shut her up."

I remain looking unblinkingly at him. "You're here because you attacked Wesley. After he attacked you."

"You *saw*?" I nod. "And didn't think about helping?"

"Actually, no. That never crossed my mind," I say truthfully. "I'll be your witness and explain."

He snorts derisively. "Makes no difference. This is my fourth 'offense' and I'm never believed."

"But the other supes who the gang attack? Even if they shouldn't fight back, don't they say anything?"

"Too scared." Grayson blows air into his cheeks and rests back, crossing one leg over his other knee. "If I think Wes and his assholes are about to attack a girl, I step in."

"Very noble."

"Are you taking the piss, Violet?"

"No. I'm saying that's a noble act," I reply indignantly.

"Hard to tell with you."

"Good." I straighten my long skirt. "Four times and they haven't expelled you?"

"Why sound disappointed?" he retorts.

"Good grief. Calm down. I'm *disappointed* because I'd want to get expelled for allegedly attacking another student."

"They won't, for the same reason as me. Our families want us here and have control over the school through their positions."

"A *Petrescu* has influence? After everything your relative did?"

"A *Blackwood* has influence? After everything *your father* did?"

I pull a tight smile and look the other way.

The door to the office opens and Mrs. Lorcan throws me a filthy look before tersely telling me to walk inside.

"LESS THAN A DAY AND YOU'RE *ALREADY* IN TROUBLE FOR YOUR self-control slipping." Mr. Willis raps his fingers on the table as I stand before them, hands behind my back. I'm accustomed to this type of meeting with school authorities, hopefully this one ends with the result I want.

"Should I tell you what happened, or is there no point?" I say and look at Mrs. Lorcan.

"We're examining Holly's injuries and will draw our conclusions then." She's pissed, angrily shuffling papers around and occasionally glaring. "I promised the academy that your parentage would not affect your behavior and that students are safe."

"They are!" I protest. "I want to leave, so I was creating a blood rune. Holly walked in and stopped me for benevolent reasons and then took hold of the item that I used to cut myself with. The only injury is on her palm."

I'm confused when Mrs. Lorcan smiles. "Oh, sweet Violet. The academy is warded against magical entry or exit. Nobody—and nothing—can find its way in or out through spells."

"Even a Blackwood's?" I retort.

She smirks as she continues to straighten her papers. "You'd obviously try blood magic, so your mother and father created some *extra* protection."

"*What?*" I half-shout. Right. I am *not* going home. I'll find somewhere else to live. Ethan would take me in. "That's nasty."

"And apparently necessary." Mrs. Lorcan's smile doesn't leave her smug face.

I suck my lips together as I stare through the arched window behind them. "Then you believe my story? Check my room. You'll find the rune."

"Somebody already did," says Mr. Willis gruffly. "There wasn't a rune."

"But..." Who removed that? Wesley or his friends?

"Violet needs moving from Darwin House," he says firmly.

"There's no other room for Violet," retorts Mrs. Lorcan. "And the Blackwoods don't want their daughter segregated. The idea is for her to become a touch more amiable to others."

I snort a laugh. "Were those my father's words?" She nods. "When he was my age, Dorian intimidated the entire school and declared himself king of the academy. Killed if they stepped out of line. Allegedly. He expects his daughter to be *amiable*?"

Mr. Willis straightens further. "Are you implying you'll do the same?"

"No. I don't kill." I wrinkle my nose. "Not *deliberately*."

An imperceptible shake of Mrs. Lorcan's head silences me. "See. I have concerns," says Mr. Willis.

No. What if Holly is the only bearable roommate? At least she isn't antagonistic.

"I solemnly promise not to tear any throats, nor remove hearts, or other body parts from humans." I cross my arms. "But if Holly would rather I roomed elsewhere, so be it."

"She needs some discipline, Mrs. Lorcan," he says. "Take away Violet's rights to leave campus for town visits."

"Considering Violet tried to leave us, and we don't want to explain to her father what happened if she does, that's a sensible idea."

My scalp prickles with irritation. "Banned from leaving campus?"

Mr. Willis leans back in his chair. "I don't want trouble, Violet Blackwood."

"I'm sure Wesley can continue his spying."

"He doesn't spy on you," says Mrs. Lorcan

"So, you believe he's romantically interested in me? Because the boy always seems to be close by. Unless he's planning to assault me like the other girls he attacks?"

Mr. Willis blinks. "Don't be ridiculous."

I tip my chin. "Bullies always get what they deserve."

"Like your father who got *dominion* over your world?"

"Let's stop this," says Mrs. Lorcan hastily. "I'm sorry, Violet. We'll review the situation again if you manage to stay out of trouble with other students."

"I intend to stay away from everybody. This place is a bigger Hell than the last."

As I leave, I can't shake Mr. Willis's last comment. His stress on 'dominion'—the name of those who fought against the old ruling council before our world was revealed. This isn't the first time I've heard whispers that Dorian Blackwood joined the Dominion terrorists in retaliation for his time at Ravenhold. Whispers that question his suitability as leader of the *new* council.

My father was allied with neither Dominion nor the ruling Confederacy back in the day. When will people realize that Dorian only follows one person's agenda?

His own.

Chapter Nine

I SPEND the day moving class to class, marveling at how mundane a supernatural academy can be. Most classes match those I attended at the human school, which I don't understand at first. Then I discover that the Houses spend a lot of time on lessons specific to their race.

More segregation, although I do understand that a mental magic class is beyond human capability and most supes don't need to study art. Mental magic isn't on the timetable today, which is a shame. I'm looking forward to some minor mind control.

Poor Holly spent most of the morning profusely apologizing until I was on the verge of using one of those minor mental magic spells to shut her up. Does the girl often apologize for another's actions? I won't even apologize for my *own*. Humans continue to confuse me.

Holly also makes a huge show of our relationship being 'normal' for roommates and emphasizing that she isn't concerned I'll murder her when she's asleep. The problem is, she's protesting to the degree that people *will* think I've charmed her. Nice that she believes everybody should be kind to one another, but does Holly understand that the world doesn't work in that way?

Still, everybody does seem to like the girl to the extent that I'd believe *she* had mind altering skills.

We attend art class, where we're taught by a human teacher—a woman with pixie cut black hair and too much enthusiasm. A very *pointless* art class that involves drawing boxes. *Boxes.* To 'learn perspective'. What's an art class without paint? There're easels and all manner of art supplies, yet we're stuck at double-desks with a black pencil. I look at the drawer marked *charcoal* and debate whether to liven the place up by drawing a runic spell or two.

"I hear that students are allowed into the town," I say to Holly as we work.

"Some of us visit after classes finish, yes. Friday night we get together with the kids who live in town." She carefully draws a wobbly line. "Crap."

"If you took that ridiculous fluffy thing from the top of your pencil, that might help," I comment and savagely draw a straight line across my own paper.

Holly shakes her head and ignores me before continuing. Poking her tongue out assists with her drawing. Marginally.

"Can you take me into town with you?" I ask.

She pauses and looks up at me from beneath her curls. "You told me you're banned from leaving campus."

"And?"

"I couldn't," she whispers. "I don't want to lose my privileges. There's this guy in town who I meet and–"

I groan. "Please don't elaborate."

"Well, I can only meet up with him a couple of times a week." She doodles on the corner of her page. "I don't want to lose that time together."

"But you endlessly send messages to each other." I point at the phone.

"That's not the same as *being* with each other. Face to face. And–"

"Again, stop." I tap my pencil on the table. "I won't bother you. I'd like to acquaint myself with the local area."

"You speak very strangely," she comments.

"And that surprises you?"

"What do you want to 'acquaint' yourself with?" she asks.

"Solace." Blank look. "Peace. The hormones in this environment choke me on every level."

"Then why do you want to be around *more* humans?" she asks.

"There are places humans don't often go. I'll find somewhere."

"Like a graveyard?" she asks in hushed tones.

"*Really*, Holly?"

"You're a..." She trails off and lowers her voice. "You know."

"Necromancer?" I ask loudly. The teacher glances up at me and I smile sweetly. "Do you think I'm about to drag people from their graves and create an army of zombies?"

The chatter that accompanied the students' scintillating activity dies.

"No," she whispers. "Sorry."

"Even the freshly buried would be no use," I continue. "More than a day and it's difficult. A greater risk of brain damage, too. Plus, there's the issue of digging them out."

Is it wrong that I'm loving the horror I've painted on the faces around me?

Holly eyes me nervously. "You're kidding, right?"

I splay my fingers on the desk, revealing perfectly painted black nails. "Do these look like the hands of somebody who digs in the earth?"

"Fucking weirdo," says a voice from the front of class.

I sigh deliberately loudly. "How did I guess you'd have an

intelligent and pertinent contribution to the discussion, Wesley?"

"Settle down. Five minutes until class ends. Anybody who hasn't completed the task because they're too busy chatting can stay behind to finish." Ms. Reynolds throws a pointed look at me.

"Crap. No." Holly starts to scrawl a wonky box.

"Are you headed into town straight after class?" I ask.

"Um. No. Maybe." Holly avoids my eyes and I purse my lips before subtly poking around in her mind.

The guy she mentioned features heavily—slightly older, tanned but blond, and an exuberant smile to match hers. I flick past before anything physical between them appears. She's picturing leaving campus, and I follow the route in her mind. A bus stop.

I feel sorry for Violet. It must be hard to have no friends, and I know she's only pretending that she doesn't care. I'm going to help. I don't care that Violet's weird. I like her.

I blink and pull out of her far too shiny thoughts.

Violet Blackwood *is* her pet project.

Task complete, I drop the pencil onto the desk and shove back my chair to stand before approaching the teacher. A foot pushes out and I pause, teeth clenched as I look at Wesley's long leg protruding in my way.

"Have you not graduated from kindergarten yet?" I ask evenly. He sneers and I crane my head to view his paper. "Isn't this a little advanced for you? Surely you need to learn to color between the lines first?"

A snicker ripples around the room, and his look turns venomous. Jumping to his feet, Wesley snatches the paper from my hand and rips my assignment in half. The paper flutters to the desk and he smirks at me.

"I guess you'll be staying behind to complete your assignment." He takes his from the desk to give to Ms.

Reynolds, but that's unfortunately impossible because the paper is now on fire.

He shrieks like a kid and drops the paper, chairs beside him screeching as the students move away from the smoldering page. Before the fire can spread anywhere, I slam my palm down on top of the flames, looking him dead in his panicked eyes.

Fire doesn't hurt me—something that gives me an edge over full-blooded vamps.

"I guess you're staying too, Wesley," I say sweetly.

Nearby, Leif screws his paper into a ball and deftly throws it into the trash.

I'M DISAPPOINTED FOR TWO REASONS.

One, Ms. Reynolds doesn't send me to the headteachers, which means I can't add this to my list of misdemeanors.

Two, if I don't get out of here soon, I can't follow Holly to the town or persuade her to take me.

Why didn't I resist the opportunity to embarrass the asshole? I glare at the back of his thick head, where he's forced to sit at the front of the classroom with a fresh sheet of paper.

I'm two rows behind, with Leif two desks away on my right. A couple of grumbling girls sit at the back. See, too much socialization *does* cause issues. If they hadn't been chatting inanely about the vampires they're 'hot for', the pair would be prettying themselves to meet those vampires by now.

Seriously. What *is* the point in friendship? Social connections distract. Have no relevance. I saw enough at the human school to see how distracted the kids were and the constant emotion filling the air screwed with my head.

Literally, because I'd pick up everything mentally and my mind was becoming mush.

I'm not losing my mind to, or over, anybody.

I admire the teacher's belief that keeping me at choking distance from the delightful Wesley would prevent anything else untoward happening. I'm perfectly capable of casting all manner of spells that would reach him.

Head down, hair flopping forward, Leif casually sketches the box, ignoring us both. Was he unhappy with his original illustration and that's why he threw it in the trash? I side glance him as I chew my pencil, considering a mind control spell on Ms. Reynolds so we can escape.

Leif doesn't fit. Yes, he's more human than shifter, but he looks older than his eighteen years and, like a lot of male shifters, Leif's taller than an average guy. I struggle to see his eyes beneath the curls. Hiding them? Are they inhuman? As a fellow hybrid and daughter with two shifter fathers, I'm intrigued.

As if aware of my scrutiny, Leif looks over, peering at me from beneath his hair, then looks at the back of Wesley's head. The pencil snaps in his hand and he quickly shoves it into a pocket before pulling out a second.

"Done." Wesley's chair loudly scrapes on the tiles, and he approaches Ms. Reynolds before slamming the paper onto her desk. "I'll be speaking to my father about your failure to reprimand the witch."

"Hybrid," I call out.

"Oh, that's right. You're also a vampire. As Holly knows."

He's tedious. I return to my illustration. A second pencil drops to Leif's desk, and I wait for him to stand too. Instead, he links hands behind his head and watches the clock tick on the wall above Ms. Reynolds. The one she keeps glancing at.

"I want those on my desk before tomorrow," she eventually says. "I have better places to be."

"As do I," I mutter.

Ms. Reynolds leaves the door ajar when she exits, and I sink back in my seat. "*This* is the way to educate humans? Drawing freaking boxes?"

"Discipline," says Leif. "Boring us shitless since nobody will attend meditation classes."

"This academy is pointless," I say and practically slice through the paper with a pencil stroke.

"Wait until we have our mixed classes." He smirks. "That's fun."

"Fun is not a word I'd use to describe this place." I toss the pencil to one side.

"Or anything at all?"

"True. Why are you here?"

"Is that a philosophical question, Wednesday?"

I fight frowning. "Who?"

"That's what the humans call you."

"Oh? I thought 'freak' and 'goth girl' were the monikers they'd chosen."

He laughs and drags his chair across to my desk, way too far into my personal space. "Why do you hide beneath your words and your black?"

"Why are you here *in this room*? You finished ten minutes ago."

Leif slides my paper across and takes the pencil, quickly completing my half-assed attempt. "Because you need my help."

"To draw a box?"

He shakes his head. "No. To help *you*. If you help me."

"You apparently misunderstand my lack of benevolence, Leif."

"I understand that you want to go to town, but due to your behavior you can't. I'll help." He hands me the pencil. "If you help me when we arrive."

"Help with what?" I ask suspiciously.

"Leaving."

Finally, he piques my interest. "Thornwood?" He nods.

"Once we leave the academy, your blood runes will work. *That's* why they're not allowing you to leave campus."

"I'd already figured that out. And don't bother asking; I won't take you with me."

Leif stands and takes both our papers. "Then you can't be *that* desperate to leave."

"Can't you take a bus from town?" I ask.

"I wouldn't get far enough, quickly enough."

"Far enough for what?"

Silently, he walks to the desk and places the papers down before heading to the door. Leif pauses and looks back at me. "Far enough that they won't catch me, Violet Blackwood."

I scoff to myself as he walks away. The guy could walk straight off campus and catch a bus to wherever he likes. There's no reason anybody would want to catch him.

Is there?

Chapter Ten

I TOYED with the idea of leaving campus anyway, but there're teachers taking unsubtle evening walks close to all the academy ground's exits. Ignoring them, I head back to Darwin House.

If I want solitude, I now have this in spades. The place is silent, the common room I've thus avoided empty—if any student did stay behind, they're tucked away in their dorm rooms.

Back at my room, I wrinkle my nose at the heavy perfume in the air, immediately walking across to light my rosemary candles to change the scent and aura. Did Leif go to town anyway? Holly obviously did.

The latest book I borrowed from the library yields nothing apart from unpleasant comments about Blackwood witches. Dorian is Blackwood by blood only, but keeps the name. He's the only one left now, apart from some old guy who doesn't bother with spells any more.

There're a few notes scrawled in the book's margins, and I look closer. These are in blue pen, but this book is over a hundred years old.

Interesting.

I copy some of the notes, but this is either a code or a foreign language.

Hmm.

Night descends on the gloom-filled evening, and I again debate whether to leave campus. Knowing my luck, the staff are still 'taking a walk'. How long am I imprisoned for? Will I need to strike a bargain with Leif to escape one night?

I'm in the bath, surrounded by more candles, reading a novel rather than history, when I hear the door creak open and then click closed. Closing the book, I toss it onto the floor and brace myself for a hearty Holly hello.

Nothing.

Holly would definitely make a noise, even if it's only firing up her laptop to watch shows about teenagers arguing. The bathroom door is locked and my pajamas on my bed. Crap. Water sloshes as I stand and cooler air hits my skin. I cover myself with a towel and move to the doorway, debating what to do.

If this is Wesley, I won't hold back on my retaliation to his invading my privacy.

But I'm hardly imposing when wrapped in a blue towel that only reaches my knees.

I press my ear to the door—no sound apart from something shuffling around. The floorboards creak, but the invader remains.

Screw this. I've enough magic to knock the person into next week. And screw the consequences.

I yank open the bathroom door, fire already at my fingertips as I stride out. A male figure crouches on the floor close to my bed.

I bloody knew it.

"What the hell are you doing, asshole?" I shout.

He falls onto his backside, revealing the trunk of magic items I brought with me. *Open.*

"I thought you'd be with Holly in town." The scruffy guy gapes at me before struggling to his feet.

Rowan? "You thought wrong." The flames flare as I stroke my palm, creating a ball. "Ten seconds to tell me what you're doing before I hit you with this."

"You don't know much about me, do you?" Rowan flicks his fingers and matching flames appear.

I sneer. "I'll mind control you to singe your own dick."

"No sudden moves or your towel might fall off, Violet." His gaze roves up my legs in a deliberate way before meeting my eyes again.

"Don't try and screw with me, Rowan," I say. "Tell me what you're doing in my room. In my trunk."

"I wanted to borrow something." He's casual, flicking the flames higher on his fingers.

"I believe borrowing without permission is classed as stealing." I nod at the bed. "On there."

He cocks his head. "Why, Violet. We hardly know each other. Surely we should have one date before a physical union."

I choke. "I mean, drop whatever you're stealing onto my bed."

As he steps forward, I slam enough magic into his head that he staggers into the wall, the fire magic dissipating from his hand.

Then hold him there, taking slow steps across the room as he struggles to move. "Is the item in your pocket? Give it to me."

I hold out a now flame-free palm.

"I never had a chance to find what I wanted." Rowan attempts to pull himself from the wall and I magically slam his head back, too. "Crap. Violet. Stop."

"Not so cocky now, huh?" I growl out, then step closer. I'm near enough to draw Rowan's magic energy away and apparently near enough that he's worried about my teeth as I bare them. "What did you want to take?"

His eyes move from my face to where the towel ties around my chest, and his interest suggests he's imagining more than he'll ever see.

"Do you have any belladonna?" he asks.

"Don't you think the school would confiscate that?"

"You look cute without make-up."

The out of the blue comment knocks my magic momentarily, and he pulls himself from the wall. I hold my ground, ready to strike. "What do you need the belladonna for?"

"A spell."

"What spell?"

"A necessary one."

"Stop being obtuse."

He moistens his lips, apparently interested in mine. I rub them. What's on my mouth? I haven't brushed my teeth yet.

"Some people should get what they deserve," he says softly. "And I intend to help with that."

"Are you referring to me?"

Light from the hallway floods the room along with Holly's singing. Which cuts short. "Oh. Umm." Dipping her head, Holly turns to leave.

"No. Stay," I call out. "Rowan didn't get what he wanted and so he's leaving."

She turns, eyes wide. "He didn't?"

"No. Not this time." Why is Rowan laughing? I spike a bolt of energy between his eyes, and he winces and swears.

"Leave," I snap.

With a mock bow, he saunters across the room, Holly

watching as if I'd invited a small demon into the room. "You're brave, sharing with her," he says.

"I had no choice, and I don't care," she retorts. "And if you do anything to Violet, you'll answer to me."

"Wow." I shake my head. "*Nobody* at this academy really understands me and what I'm capable of. Holly, nobody would dare do anything."

Rowan pokes his tongue against his top teeth. "Uh huh. Well, good night sweet Violet."

The magic I mentally throw at him fails to hit, colliding with the closing door instead. "Rowan needs to watch his back," I say with disgust.

"What's happening?" Holly pulls off her jacket and carefully folds it over a chair. "We're not supposed to invite guys into our rooms. I mean, obviously people do but—"

"Rowan let himself in."

"That's worrying. The guy's... odd."

"I don't think he'll be back," I reply. "And if he has any sense, he'll stay away from me." The open trunk catches mine and Holly's eye. "I need to ward that. Dumb of me not to."

"What's inside?" she asks.

"Things another witch should keep his sticky fingers off of." I kick the trunk closed. "How was your trip?"

"Are you interested?"

"No. But I'm coming with you next time." I grab my pajamas from the bed and stalk back into the bathroom. A fresh-faced, wet-haired Violet taunts me from the mirror.

Cute.

Seriously?

Chapter Eleven

Neither Rowan nor Wesley bother me the next morning, since neither guy is at breakfast—which I reluctantly agree to attend. I don't miss the whispering and filthy looks from his group of hangers on both at breakfast and as we stand outside a room ready for history class, so I ask my auburn-haired, local news channel why.

"Wes isn't well," she says.

"Too much to drink?"

Holly draws me to one side. "What were you *really* doing last night when the building was empty?"

"Reading. Bathing. Repelling thieving witches." I frown. "Why?"

"Wesley found runes in his room last night. The witch professor called to inspect them confirmed they're designed to mess with someone's mind." She bites her lip. "Has Wes gotten under your skin that much?"

"What runes? I want to see them."

"Nobody can go inside. The room is being cleansed, or whatever witches do."

"And Wesley?"

She shakes her head. "Under observation for 'erratic behavior'."

"And everybody thinks *I* did this?" I scowl.

"You have clashed with him a lot, and you used a blood rune yesterday morning."

"I don't hide what I do to people. Ever." I glance at the humans passing by who mutter at me. Some witches and vamps whisper, one or two nodding and smiling at me. "Oh no. Please don't tell me this situation has increased my popularity."

Grayson appears at the top of the stairs and, noticeably, some humans shuffle away from him. He's managed to find his uniform again today and his eyes are brighter green, although I take care not to look too closely. There's an identifiable glow about him. He's hemia—has he been indulging in blood?

"Nice one, Violet," he says.

"Nice what?"

"Wesley." He grins. "Next time, put Wes out of action for longer. I heard he'll be back to normal by the afternoon. Shame."

"I didn't do anything," I protest. "Doesn't anyone have a photo of these runes?"

"Blood runes?" says a voice behind. "I saw them." Kirsten, one of the girls who's often attached to Wesley, strides over and looks down her long nose at me, blue eyes hard. "According to Professor Wren, only one person can use blood runes—you."

"What?" I nod at the phone in her shaking hand. "Show me." Kirsten holds the phone up, screen outwards. Yes, there're blood runes on the floor in the image, but they look nothing *like* a Blackwood rune. "They're not mine and don't look harmful."

Kirsten gawks. "Um, Wes is in the infirmary."

"And does Wesley enjoy amateur dramatics?" I ask. She gives me a blank look. "He's pretending. Someone is trying to set me up."

Bloody Rowan. Literally. He was definitely in Darwin House last night. But why would he do that to me?

"Do I go to the heads' office, or wait until I'm summoned?" I ask Holly.

"Wait?" she suggests.

"Hmm." I carefully study the students gathered outside the classroom. "Do all races attend this class? Everybody in our year?"

"Yes. Learning each other's history is important for society moving forward," Holly says solemnly.

"Hmm," I repeat. No Rowan, so I can't throttle the truth out of him. "I should visit someone."

And I don't mean Mrs. Lorcan and Mr. Willis.

DOES ANYBODY BOTHER LOOKING FOR ME OR DO STUDENTS often skip class? Because I spend most of the morning in the library again. I spent my formative years on an island with my fugitive parents, until the world became more accommodating, which adds to my desire for solitude. Books are my solace and I enjoy studying historical tomes for any hidden meanings or spells, which heightens my desire for Rowan's book.

I've already created my own nook, including a deep purple cushion that I've shoved against the wall at the end of a set of shelves, a growing stack of books becoming a barrier around my den. I'll endeavor to spend as much time as I can here and as little as possible in class. If I'm leaving, there's no point in attending.

I curl up on the cushion and read one of the books I tried

to take from the library last night. The librarian caught me before I could leave. Sneaky witch and her magical senses. The book was located on the same shelf as Rowan's precious one, and again, this book has notes scrawled in the margins. When I turn to the last page, I discover someone drew runes with the same foreign words written beneath.

They're not runes I recognize, and I've studied every witch family.

This foreign language begins to annoy me too.

Or is this code? Then I need to make a note and figure this out but copying the whole page will take forever. Taking a photo would be easier but I don't have a camera. Anywhere. I grit my teeth—if I possessed a cellphone, I would, but I don't.

Why would I? I've no desire to be drawn further into others' lives, nor am I particularly fond of cats, and phones appear to contain an abundance of feline images. Then there's the small faces and mysterious tiny pictures. If I were superstitious, I'd believe we'd returned to a time of witchcraft where cats were worshipped as familiars, and witches communicated with secret symbols.

I'm not superstitious, but this has added to my aversion.

Now? I wish I did possess one if only for the camera.

Wrinkling my nose, I pull a pen and paper from my bag and copy the first circular symbol. Close to Blackwood, but not quite. The intersecting lines aren't precise enough. I scrawl down as many of the annoying words as I can, then fold and tuck the paper away.

Is somebody attempting to perform Blackwood magic? Because this is similar to the rune the girl showed me, but not close enough. Rowan? Re-shelving the book, I run fingers back and forth along the row, eyes closed, in case other magic attracts me.

Ley lines converge at the academy—another reason the supernatural school was rebuilt here—and as with most

Thornwood academies, that convergence happens beneath the main building, often the library.

No magic leaps from any particular book, so I pick up the next in the row. I'm about to sit again when I hear two male voices. Nobody else approached this musty part of the library in the hours that I've sat here, or since I saw Rowan. Could my wait be over?

I shuffle towards the end of the shelves, squeezing myself between the books and the wall, before pulling one out to give me a small window to watch through.

Rowan, as I thought.

And Leif?

They're both in uniform, Rowan as crumpled as ever, and Leif's blazer stretched tight across his broad back. Seems they don't make them *quite* big enough for half-shifters, but at least they gave him pants that reach his ankles.

The few times I've seen Rowan around campus, students kept at a distance, and he seemed oblivious to their reaction to him. I wouldn't pick Leif as someone he'd be friendly with. Leif speaks in a low urgent tone, while Rowan stands opposite with a closed expression. Once Leif stops speaking, Rowan holds his gaze for a moment before crossing to the shelves close to me.

Stealing books again? I shrink back.

"You told me you're capable," says Leif, voice hushed. "Why won't you help?"

"Because."

"Because what?"

Typical Rowan vagueness.

"Because we need a better plan." Rowan examines the row of books closely. "More practice."

"I don't have time," Leif retorts. "The situation needs dealing with."

Rowan turns. "Yes. But there'll be consequences. Are you prepared for that?"

"I'll get away from here before anybody knows what's happened," Leif replies urgently. "That's why I need your help."

"Consequences for *me*."

"Your family will protect you if there's any fallout, Rowan."

"And you'll spend life as a fugitive?" He shakes his head. "There're other solutions we can try."

"No!" Leif's voice rises and I startle. "I've protected you. Helped you. This was our bargain."

Rowan sighs before turning back to pull out another book. "I said, I need more practice. This isn't my usual magic. There're things I need."

"Like what?"

Yes, Rowan. Like what? Something from Violet's trunk?

"Stuff." He shakes the book at Leif. "I'm almost there. Are you headed to the fire tonight?"

"Yeah."

"I'm coming."

Leif falls quiet for a moment. "Are you sure?"

"Don't worry. I won't get involved with their bullshit. Not unless *you* pull me in."

"Not interested in their games. No, you'll need to meet me somewhere else. I don't want to be seen with you," Leif replies.

"Charming. Perhaps I don't want to be seen with *you*, Leif."

"When this goes down, if people know we're friends, then they'll know you're involved. Do you really want that, *Rowan*?"

"Graveyard."

There's a pause before Leif utters an incredulous, "What?"

"Meet me there."

This is more interesting than Rowan's bibliophilia. Is grave dirt needed for Rowan's spell? Their bickering continues and I step back before Rowan makes his way any further along the shelves. The conversation ends and the space around falls silent again as they wander away.

Looks like *I'm* going to this mysterious fire tonight. And the graveyard, too. Well, I've not checked the place out yet and I always acquaint myself with the dead.

Chapter Twelve

HOLLY HANDS me a cerise pink quilted jacket with a white fur-lined hood. The monstrosity would reach my knees if I wore it. She nods. "You'll need different color leggings and different boots to your usual."

"Don't you have anything less..." I hold the coat at arm's length. "Pink."

"Hang on." She roots around in her extensive wardrobe and pulls out a fluffy blue cropped jacket. "This? It's shorter, so you'd need to wear something to match. If you wear the pink one, that'll cover more of you."

My teeth grind. "Fine. But why not my usual black leggings?"

"Don't you want to blend in?"

"In *this*?" I choke. "I'll be a beacon."

But Holly already set out three pairs of legging in various primary colors. One with embroidered hearts, another with roses, and one with stars. "Holly..." I groan.

"Hearts." She smirks as she holds up the yellow pair.

I glare and grab the navy blue leggings. "Stars."

The smirk grows as Holly rummages again, then holds up

another two items. She's loving this. "And these boots are cute."

"There's white fur around the ankles," I say tersely.

"It's not real."

"There's *fur*. And they're *also* pink."

"Right." Holly drops the offending boots to the floor. "Stay at the academy tonight. I'm only trying to help."

When Holly offered to assist me in leaving for the evening, I'd pictured her showing me a little-known way through the fence.

But not this.

How desperately do I want to discover Rowan and Leif's plans? Especially as the fire they spoke about is a weekly get together for both students and local kids, which gives me the chance to watch how they interact. I'll work out which kids to avoid. Holly tells me there's alcohol involved and plenty of 'intermingling'. The academy and local authorities turn a blind eye because this helps foster closer relations between the academy and town.

A lot closer in some cases, apparently.

Teeth still clenched, I pick up the items and cross the room to change.

"Shame your face will be hidden under the hood; I could've completed your makeover. You have such pretty blue eyes. Unless you want—"

"No," I interrupt as I pull the coat belt tight around my waist. "I already look like a unicorn threw up on me."

"I do have some leggings with rainbows if—" My hard look cuts her short. She tips her head, and a ghost of a smile plays on her lips. "Be careful. The boots have heels. You don't want to face-plant."

I eye my Docs. I wouldn't be the only student wearing *those*. "I could—"

Holly frowns. "No. And a 'thank you' would be nice. I could be in trouble for *helping* you."

Sitting on the edge of the bed, I pull on the shiny pink boots. "Thank you. I'm appreciative even though I don't like your methods. And if anybody does blame you, I'll just tell them I used my mind control and then ensured you forgot."

Holly doesn't respond, and I glance up. She's wary, the smile gone. "Would you do that to me?"

I carefully consider my answer. *If necessary, yes.* "No."

Holly sits on her bed, chewing on her thumbnail. "Can I ask you something about your magic?"

"I can't teach humans any spells."

She shakes her head. "No. The necromancy. Do you do that often? There're rumors you created zombies at your old school." I frown. "Mice zombies."

"Oh, that." I wave a hand. "Animals are easy."

She pauses and gives me a long look I don't understand, so I lean down to fasten the boots.

Holly's one student who never appears fazed by what or who I am, which makes life easier around the academy. She's popular but doesn't have the superior nature I'd expect with that popularity, and I'm amused when I hear her stand up for me on occasion.

I appreciate her not freaking out after the whole blood incident, but I've never known somebody to trust me before. Mostly because I've never known many people my age. I *am* concerned about the thoughts I caught in her mind. Holly doesn't understand me as well as she thinks.

"Did you grow up in a castle?" she asks.

Is she serious? I look up. "Like Dracula? No. My parents have an estate in Scotland."

"Sorry, that sounded silly." She smiles. Another long pause. "What do you mean animals are easy?"

I sigh. "I spent my early years alone on an island with my

family and made friends with the local wildlife. The animals died. Nobody hurt them, although one or two no doubt found themselves victims in the food chain. I couldn't cope. I wanted them back, so I brought them back to life." I say and she gawks despite my matter-of-fact story.

But I did want them so, so badly—they were my friends. My emotional response tuned into the necromancy and my wish came true. At the time, I had no idea how I reanimated corpses, but it happened. Another reason to teach me to control emotions—accidental necromancy.

"I wasn't supposed to use the magic. My parents didn't suspect anything at first, until they noticed how the wildlife became unusually obedient and would follow me everywhere. Even batter at my window if I locked them outside the house."

Holly snorts a laugh. "Did you have birds fluttering around your head and rabbits at your feet?"

"Sometimes."

"Violet, the little Disney princess!" she exclaims.

I half-smile too. "Sure, if you discount that princess's fascination with blood magic. Hardly Disney."

As Holly continues to chuckle to herself, I'm confused that this is her reaction to my story. Shouldn't she be freaked out?

"Maybe Snow White was a necromancer?" she suggests.

"Perhaps some kind of witch. She did have seven men and witches have consorts. Thankfully, my mother stopped at three; seven fathers would be hell," I say seriously. "And then there's the prince dislodging apple from her throat. *Please*. The woman was dead for years. *He* was evidently a particularly skilled necromancer. Disney princes and princesses? Bonded witches."

"Oh, bonded witches are a nightmare," says Holly and grimaces. "Upset one, and the other goes feral."

"They can't help that behavior. Once they meet and connect, the witches would kill to protect each other."

Holly straightens. "I didn't know they'd go that far!"

"Under severe provocation." I shrug. "Nothing anyone can't do."

"Are your parents bonded?"

"They're… different. Maybe. They have each other's blood. She died and he—" Holly blanches. She can't *talk* about blood either? "Did vampire stuff."

"Right."

"So, the unfortunate incident at my last high school resulted from my disgust at humans mistreating animals, Holly. I still need practice, so you can imagine what the mice looked like as they dragged themselves around the classroom."

She stares. Again. Is she about to vomit?

Instead, Holly bites her lip and lowers her voice. "Do you have any human pets, or were you joking?"

"I'm still practicing on animals. I won't try humans until I'm more skilled since the results can vary. I've enough dealing with living humans; I don't want ones tied to me by magic."

I don't want tying to anybody at all.

"I'm also respecting my mother's wishes. I haven't told anybody else at the academy, Holly."

Holly nods and stands. "Thank you for trusting me. But if the students worry that you want to collect a group of mindless teen followers, they'll keep away. You won't make friends."

"Precisely. Besides, I don't need to create 'zombies' to collect mindless teen followers. Most are halfway there already."

She sighs before the smile returns and she pulls on the blue jacket that she offered me earlier. "Well, tonight will be fun! I bet you've never been to anything like this before."

Fun. *Debatable.* But I need to find Rowan's secret.

"And the surroundings are dark?" I ask. "I'd rather stay in the shadows."

Holly takes her phone from the nightstand. "One day at a time, I guess."

"Until what?"

"Until you learn how to *have* fun."

"I have my own amusements, Holly." I take the paper I wrote the mysterious words on and tuck it into the coat pocket. "I'm visiting the graveyard first."

Holly pauses in answering the message on her phone and looks up. "I didn't think you were serious about that. I can never tell if you're joking."

"I don't tell jokes."

"Even though you're funny."

"What?"

Holly shrugs. "The things you say."

"Then you have an odd sense of humor."

She shakes her head and goes back to her messaging.

I consider myself heartless and have no desire to integrate with people, but I'd argue my love of animals makes up for that. Is this a necromancy thing? A disconnect from people that stops us from wanting to save everybody we feel deserves help?

Ha. As if necromancy comes from the heart—those who do use the magic do so for their own ends, not because they can't bear to lose someone. And a reanimated creature isn't a mindless zombie. Often they've all their old memories and aren't aware what's happened to them.

But they are under the necromancer's mental control. How can that not tempt me?

Chapter Thirteen

YOUNGER STUDENTS also join the older, which makes me less noticeable when I skulk at the back of the bus with Holly. She chose the pink leggings with red hearts to add more color to her outfit, and then covered her fingers in red-gemmed silver rings, her brightness overshadowing mine. I turn towards the window, hood pulled over my face, watching the retreating academy surrounded by a fiery evening sky.

"What time does this event start?" I ask.

"Start? It's not a meeting. Just whenever people arrive after dark," she replies. "I can't wait for you to meet Ollie."

"Hmm." I examine my black fingernails. At least they survived the pink-fest. "Where's the graveyard? Far from the bus stop?"

"I'm not sure I should let you go to the graveyard alone."

I pull a disparaging face. "I don't need anybody's protection. Unless... Are you worried I lied, and I'll bring my army of zombies to your party?"

"Ha ha. No. Just be careful."

"The biggest threat to my health is this coat, which is suffocating me."

"Loosen the buttons." She reaches out to help, and I shuffle away. "And promise you'll meet me outside the park gates by eight. Do you know where that is?"

"The bus passed them." I gesture. "That way."

She nudges me. "I hope you have fun at the graveyard."

This time, I spot the teasing and smile. "Always."

THE BUS HALTS AT A STOP CLOSE TO A SHOPPING MALL AND I shudder as the dazzling, uninviting lights beckon in the students, swallowing them into a nightmare that will suck away their souls. Money. Whatever.

Holly knows my thoughts on stores, which gives me a valid reason to partake in my own activities for an hour. Leif and Rowan weren't on the bus and fleetingly I worry they've decided not to come to town.

The town population may've increased over the years, and amenities to match, but there's hidden history beneath the malls and fast food places, a darker side to the bright modern world. That darkness once hid the supes and secrets, some of which remain.

The building that became one of the original Nightworld Academies existed for several hundred years, and shifters and witches lived amongst the humans in town. Vampires too, but not as many. They found it easier to hide in bigger cities.

My fascination with the vulnerability of humans and supes alike isn't the only thing that attracts me to places filled with burial sites. The history that's never written in books and instead lost with death means there're mysteries amongst the gravestones. Perhaps even an answer to the coded words and unusual runes—another reason for my visit.

Mysteries must always be solved to put the world back to

normal, such as why Rowan wants to meet Leif here. Because something in the graveyard will aid his secret spell?

The small stone church at the rear of the grounds doesn't match the rest of the town, a part of the past that fascinates me so much. Much of the graveyard contains modern headstones, many with flowers in front of the shining marble. I make my way further down the hill towards the older part, where forgotten people are buried, and trees bow in reverence, the weeping willows aptly named.

Several small mausoleums rest amongst the gravestones, and I bet if I studied them I'd recognize at least one witch family name amongst the town's founding families.

As I approach, I reach a small, circular memorial at the edge of the weathered stones, oddly positioned and out of place. Although gray, the stone is newer, and names are written in a spiral around animal footprints. I recognize birds and wolves, maybe a bear, but there're several more animals I don't.

The stone is smooth beneath my fingers as I trace over the black inlaid text. My fascination with the dead drew me to cemeteries many times over the years and I've come across memorials peculiar to witches and vampires, but never this.

Shifters? Why here in the center of the graveyard?

I ensure I'm on alert for Rowan and Leif so that I can hide again, and few can ever sneak up on me. However, *Grayson* can move fast enough that he's beside me the moment I register him approaching. I hastily stand and frown at him.

"I thought I could smell you," he says.

"That is exceptionally gross." I pull down the coat hood and blow hair from my face.

Grayson's black clothing gives him more camouflage than my rainbow attire, and he digs hands into his leather jacket pockets and peers at me through his less-shiny eyes. "Although you smell strongly of Holly, too. Her coat, I presume? You look as if you've been swallowed by a marshmallow."

"How amusing."

"Did you decide to fit in? That'll take more than clothes."

Glaring, I pull at the coat buttons and drag the thing off before bunching it in my hands. "I had to disguise myself to leave campus."

He laughs. "That's pointless. Someone will look for you."

"And I'll hide."

"Love the leggings." Grayson ignores me and nods. "And the boots. The black T-shirt spoils the pretty girl effect though."

My fingers grip the coat harder. "Any particular reason you chose to stalk me and insult me?"

"I wanted to watch the necromancer at work."

Is he serious? "I can't reanimate people who're rotted." I gesture around me. "Or bodies missing vital organs."

"Good tip." He smirks. "So, I don't need to help you dig up any bodies?"

"Why? Do you have a spade hidden beneath your edgy leather jacket?"

"I can bring one next time."

Shaking my head, I point at the strange stone. "What's this?"

"You don't know?" He crouches. "This is a memorial to the kids who died at the old academy."

"I thought that was on campus. I've seen the plaque inside the library."

"Yeah. The shifters wouldn't allow *their* kids' names on that one. The elders wanted the shifter memorial in the town." He rubs his nose. "You might've noticed shifters no longer attend."

"My fathers are trying to fix the damaged relations between shifters and other supes. I thought most shifters accepted us now? Like the humans do." Ethan works with re-integrating the mids, and Zeke's involved with a project to help restore the balance amongst more resistant elders and the younger shifters. The pair travel a lot, but I prefer when they're home because Eloise is happier, which helps the atmosphere.

"Yeah, but there're traditionalists amongst everybody—witches, vamps, or shifters. Humans too."

I consider his words, but I don't have time for this. "Why *are* you here? Looking for a human snack? You'll find more suitable candidates in town. Living ones."

"No." He buries his hands deeper in his pockets. "I wanted to talk to you."

"What about?"

"Nothing in particular."

"What's the point in that?"

"Getting to know each other."

I step back. "Excuse me? Is this about Dorian again? I'm not taking you to see him."

"No." The willows whisper in the breeze, brushing against my hair. What's happening here? "We've a couple of things in common."

"Only that we're both students at Thornwood. I have nothing in common with anybody apart from that." I tramp towards the pebbled path that leads towards the gates. Grayson's presence might stop Rowan and Leif from entering the graveyard.

"And we both hate Wes Willis," he calls after me.

Halting, I spin around. "Hating somebody takes energy. Energy they don't deserve wasted on them."

"But I bet you'd be happy if Wes wasn't here any longer." Grayson reaches me and there's a new intensity taking over his earlier teasing tone.

"Again, energy wasted. Why give him space inside my head?"

He pauses and his unusual eyes catch my attention again. "Does anybody have space inside your head, Violet?"

Will this guy ever shut up? "Do I think about people? If necessary, to work out their motivations, yes. Such as you."

Grayson doesn't respond for a moment. But he *still* doesn't leave. "You think about me?"

"At this moment, yes, because I'm trying to figure out why you're here. Usually? No. Why would I? You're not relevant."

"Oh, man." Grayson rests on a nearby gravestone. "Do you understand how unpleasant you sound sometimes?"

"Because I'm always clear to people what I think?" I shrug. "I prefer to avoid miscommunication."

"Not all communication is words, Violet. Do you ever read how people feel from their faces? Their body language?"

Irritation prickles across my skin. "If people can't say what they think and feel, that's their issue, not mine. If I'm ever interested, I can read their minds, but again, that's a waste of energy unless strictly necessary."

He pulls himself upright again and looks down at me. "You should teach yourself to read people, Violet. Treat it as a new language. One you can't learn from books."

Language. "Oh!" I delve into my pocket. If he's here, Grayson can make himself useful. "Do you know *this* language?"

As I unfold the paper, Grayson finally shuts up, but he looks as if I slapped him. "I can read expressions," I suggest. "My mother taught me."

"Man, you're weird," he says with a sigh and holds out a hand. "Show me."

As I pass the paper, his fingers brush mine and I snatch them away. *No to physical contact.* Of any kind. If Holly attempts to hug me one more time, I won't be responsible for what magic triggers.

Even without the watery light from the moon, Grayson reads without any problem. Hemia vamps may be able to walk in the day now, but their night vision remains. "What am I looking at here?"

"That's 'no'?" I take back the paper and push it into the coat pocket.

"Looks like a code."

I give a tight smile and walk away. "I'd figured that out, but I can't figure out the code."

"Where did you find this?" He catches up and walks alongside me as I head back to and along the pebbled path.

"In a book when hiding in the library, since I was bored of the scrutiny over Wesley's so-called injuries."

"People like Wes always get what they deserve."

"Not always."

"Someone who attacks other students and gets away with shit because his father is headmaster? He *should* get what he deserves." Grayson side glances me. "Don't you think?"

Please shut *up.* "I have to go now. Thank you for your explanation about the memorial," I reply, and as I walk away, I add, "Stalking is creepy, Grayson, and although I like creepy things, I'd rather you didn't."

As I pass through the gates, I frown. Why is he chuckling at me?

Chapter Fourteen

GRAYSON DOESN'T FOLLOW ME, which I'm thankful for because he's given me a headache. My irritation with him has grown because now I've missed my chance to watch Leif and Rowan. If they came to the graveyard, no way would they walk into the place if they heard or saw Grayson and me.

Shrugging on Holly's coat, I stand across the street from the mall debating what to do. Go back to the graveyard and wait? Or head to the park gates? Why didn't I ask Holly to meet me here instead?

I straighten in surprise as the pair walk from the mall. They wear dark hoodies obscuring their faces, but Leif's bulkier build beside Rowan's slimmer one assures me this is who I'm looking at.

They don't speak to each other, heads down, as they move quickly along the street in the direction I need to go. Their meeting wasn't a *meeting*, but part of a plan?

I shadow them, darting from place to place in case I need to suddenly blend in on the tree-lined street. The pair suddenly pause and move closer to the fence around the park, melding with the dark. Half a dozen guys approach from the opposite direction, obnoxiously loud and walking with purpose. Even without using my magic to sense who, I can guess.

The group veer through the tall metal park gates and I scrunch my face up. I recognize Wesley and a couple of his bone-headed friends, but there're other guys with them. Locals? Whoever they are, Wesley has an arm wrapped around one of the guy's shoulders, shouting out instructions to the others. They're already more obnoxious than usual and I can guess what's in their backpacks. Alcohol.

"Violet!" Holly waves at me from beside the same gates, close to a chain fence, where she stands with a tall blond guy. As I approach, she purses her lips. "You're late"

"Sorry. I don't have a watch. I had to guess."

She sighs. "You're so difficult."

"Grayson distracted me," I say, and look around. The gates lead into an unlit area with a child's playground a few hundred meters away. I half-expect Wesley and his gang to play on the swings, but they've walked into the dark, loud voices carrying back to us.

Holly gawks. "What were you doing with Grayson in the graveyard that distracted you?"

The guy chuckles and I frown. "Nothing. He followed me for reasons I can't fathom."

"That's a bit creepy," replies Holly.

"I have to expect creepy if I visit a graveyard. Honestly, I think Grayson wants to meet Dorian, and that's why he's bothering me. Believes if he's nice, I might introduce them."

"Sure it is," says Holly with a smile.

Is this one of the moments Grayson mentioned? I don't understand her reply. "He showed me a memorial to shifters. I didn't realize how many died."

"Yeah, that's part of the issue with the academy rebuilding

here," says the guy. "Some of the local shifter elders don't agree with the decision."

"The old world dealt with everybody responsible for the event. They're all dead. Isn't that enough?" I ask.

"Some shifters are also odd about mixing with humans," says the guy. "Conflict all round."

"How intriguing," I say.

Holly gives me a look that I *do* recognize—am I joking or not? Well, it *is* interesting. She shakes her head and links her arm through the guy's, pulling him closer. "Oh! Ollie, this is Violet. Violet—Ollie."

"I guessed from your description and the possessive way you're gripping him," I say. "And I doubt I need introducing to anybody."

"Hey, to you too." Ollie exchanges a look with Holly that tells me I definitely don't need any introduction and that he's heard plenty about me.

"Holly and Ollie. Cute. Are we going to this 'gathering'?" I ask and pass them, walking through the open gates. "How far?"

"You're very keen for somebody who doesn't like social occasions," comments Holly, as she hurries to catch up.

"I'm only here for the opportunities."

Ollie laughs again. "Opportunities with who?"

"Grayson won't be at the gathering. Vamps don't go near fire." says Holly.

"Why would that matter to me?"

Holly walks closer. "The tension was there the day you met Grayson. I can tell these things."

"'Things'?"

"A natural connection—attraction between two lost souls, but then you spoiled it with that bad aura." She sighs. "You're well suited."

I pause in horror. Lost souls? *Good grief.* "Are you

suggesting I want romantic involvement with Grayson? You say some ridiculous things, but that's the worst. If I'm not interested in making friends, why would I spend time with somebody who'd insist on touching me?"

"You might be curious?" she suggests.

"Death makes me curious. Touching makes me nauseous." I shake my head and start walking again, half-tripping on the uneven ground in these stupid boots.

I would've found my way to the exact location alone; such a large group of people are easily sensed by their smell and loud voices that hit my vampire hearing, even from a distance.

This sounds and smells like a *lot* of kids.

We're at the edge of the public, carefully tended area of the parkland, close to woods that edge the town. A small fire burns in a dip in the ground, casting more light than the obscured moon. Instantly, I'm drawn to the flames, already picturing my old fire familiar hiding in the center of the blaze. I'm suspicious whether he really *did* leave me, or if my mother used a spell to rid the world of my mischievous serpent. Mischievous, arsonist, whatever.

A group of human guys and girls sit on the ground across from us, flames flickering patterns across their faces as they chatter and drink from a bottle they're passing around. There's a pungent, woody smell that isn't from the shifters near them, but something the nearby witches are smoking.

The giggling girls pass around the witches' makeshift cigarette. A blond girl has her head on one witch's shoulder, his arm possessively around her shoulders, and I retch when the other girl blows smoke into the second guy's mouth.

People are genuinely gross.

Holly leads me to a familiar human group and, as usual, we all behave as if I'm not here, which is the best outcome. She and Ollie remove their coats and place them on the ground to sit on, and I remain standing. I'm on the edge of them all, physically and socially, following the incident with Wesley.

Wesley isn't with them, he's still with his loud, alcohol and testosterone-fueled group beneath a nearby tree. Sitting, I wrap my arms around my knees, drawing them to my chest as I survey those gathered.

No Rowan or Leif.

"There're shifters here," I say and indicate the group close to Wesley's. "And they're talking to academy kids. That contradicts what you told me."

"Not all shifters are prejudiced. There's some tension between the big shifter Viggo and human Kai from town, but Wes sensibly keeps his head down around them."

"So, Wes is only the alpha male when at school, not here? Hmm." I unfasten the coat. "Which is Kai? I've figured out Viggo—he *smells* alpha even from here."

"Is that a witch thing?" asks Ollie. "How people smell?"

"Vampire." He subtly shifts away. "Don't worry, you don't smell. I can't even scent your blood."

"Uh." He exchanges a look with Holly. "Right."

"I have... medication to prevent my bloodlust," I continue, pulling my arms from the coat sleeves, and he moves further into the shadow.

"Kai's there." Holly points to a guy in the middle of a group that're at the opposite side of the fire to the shifters. How odd they all choose to attend when they're not friendly.

"Have you seen Rowan or Leif?" I ask Holly.

She takes her mouth from the bottle she's drinking from. "They don't often come. Rowan's a bit... intense and doesn't have a lot of friends. Didn't he upset you? Leif likes to avoid the shifters. They give him crap about attending the academy."

"But it seems as if you're all socializing well. Or do the

alphas butt heads later?" I politely decline when she offers me the bottle.

"The shifters? They can get raucous but aren't usually confrontational," says Ollie.

"Oh. I meant *all* the alphas. Like Wesley and Kai."

"Kai?" Ollie leans back, palms on the ground behind him. "Sometimes. His dad's on the town council, so he's pretty much untouchable."

I tip my head, watching all their interaction. Surprisingly, the place feels tension free. "Untouchable? Sounds like someone else I know."

"You?" asks Holly.

I throw her a look. "No. Wesley. He's the headmaster's son."

"Yes, but *you're* Dorian Blackwood's daughter," replies Holly.

Ollie's expression doesn't change—this is one of the few things I liked about human school. Nobody gave a crap who I or my father was.

"He never causes trouble anyway," comments Ollie and takes the bottle from Holly. "Kai's a cool guy."

"And the shifters?" I gesture at the group on their own.

"Usually they're all friendly—there's an understanding not to interfere in each other's worlds," says Holly.

"But the undercurrent is there," says Ollie. "Viggo can get antsy when he's had a few beers, but he's harmless."

"Harmless?" I arch a brow. "He's a shifter. They're not in control a hundred percent of the time, even if they want to be."

"Viggo's too young to shift yet," says Holly. "If he became a mid, that'd be an embarrassment for his family."

I study him as well as I can from this distance—a mountain of a guy who makes Leif look like a small hill, with long hair loose around his face. Even though mids aren't ostracized like they were before the accords with humans, if someone from an important family 'let's them down' in this way, that prejudice is well and truly alive.

"Early shifting isn't always through choice. Sometimes it's from major provocation," I say. "Which could happen in the great soup of teenage hormones."

Ollie looks at me as if I'm speaking another language, then places a hand on Holly's knee, whispering in her ear. Her giggle grates like nails on a chalkboard. *Some* body language I can read very well.

"I'm going for a walk," I say and stand.

"Don't go far!" protests Holly.

"Good idea," says Ollie and trails a finger down Holly's cheek, eyes on her lips.

Ugh. Before Holly can respond, I wander away towards the fire. Ordinarily, I'd keep in the shadows, but... fire. I'm lost in focusing on the hottest part of the blaze, zoning out from those around and don't hear anything around. I'm not joking about the human soup—the atmosphere is choking my vampire senses.

As does the liquor smell on Wesley's breath as he unsubtly approaches.

Chapter Fifteen

WESLEY GLANCES at me before lifting his arm and tossing the empty bottle into the fire. Someone copies him and I eye roll at their show of... whatever they're trying to demonstrate.

"How are you feeling?" I ask him sweetly.

He scowls, eyes lit by the fire. "You need to be careful who you screw around with."

"As do you, dear Wesley." I look back to the growing flames. "And the rune wasn't mine. Nice try by whoever drew it, though."

We lapse into a welcome silence.

"Your parents are immortal," says Wesley eventually.

I pivot to face him. "I can only guess you're speaking to me since the vamps aren't here."

Flames lick his face in orange as the blaze heats the situation.

"Are *you*?" he continues.

"I don't know. I haven't died yet. Why?"

He shrugs. "Just asking."

"Were you intending to throw me into the fire to discover if I am?"

Wesley's voice lowers. "Why would I hurt you in front of witnesses?"

"Bragging rights?" I suggest.

"Yeah, well, I think even I'd get into a lot of shit if I threw someone into a fire." He sneers at me. "Shame."

"Very well. Another time then?" I suggest, capturing his eyes with mine. "But you keep failing to remember something."

My magic snakes between us, butting through the thin barrier around Wesley's mind. As expected, there's little of interest inside, the inebriation dulling his dull thoughts further. Wesley shakes his head as if dislodging something buzzing in his ear.

"I'm a powerful hybrid who could kill you from a distance —or even control your mind so *you* hurt yourself, not me." I bare my teeth at him. "You're a bully, Wesley. A sad little boy. I'm not the only one who finds your behavior unpleasant. You need to watch out; something might happen to you."

Wesley presses a palm to his head, where my mental fingernails scrape through his mind, causing pain. Not as much as he deserves, but pain anyway.

"Are you threatening me?" Wesley's voice rises and some glance at us before returning to their own activities. Evidently, outbursts by the academy bully aren't unusual. Nor are they to be interfered with.

"Good grief, no. I have no desire to waste my energy or magic on you, Wesley."

"Maybe I *should* push you into that fucking fire," he says through gritted teeth, a slur to his words.

I step nearer and tiptoe to bring our faces closer. "Try, and only one of us would get hurt. Here's a clue which one: not me."

"Your kind shouldn't be amongst us," he says, backing off and lifting his arm, pointing down at me. "You assholes fuck up our world. Now I'm forced to bloody live with you all at that fucking academy."

"Who you talking to?" calls Viggo.

"The freak. All supes are fucking freaks. You should stay away." He hiccups and stumbles as one of his friends seizes his shoulder and says something urgently. "Yeah, I do mean *all* of them."

Hush descends, leaving only the crackling fire and distant sounds of traffic before a murmur ripples through those gathered. Wesley shoots a slicing look my way and I smile.

Oh, dear. Don't you want them all to hear what you really *think?*

Wesley's eyes go wide, and he hits the side of his head again as my voice bounces around his mind.

All I'm doing is revealing his thoughts.

"Shut up," he says and slams a hand over his mouth. Is he talking to himself or me? Well, technically, this is me since I'm forcing the poisonous words from Wesley's mouth—the truth.

White light flashes across my vision, the distraction enough for my grip on Wesley to snap back and hit my own mind. I blink away the magic and look directly in the direction the spell came from.

Rowan lurks beneath a tree away from the gathering but close enough to cast spells. His face is indistinguishable in the dark, and he's alone.

What the...?

"Fucking bitch," snarls Wesley and stumbles away, shoving at his friend's hand. "She made me say that!" he calls to Viggo. "Mind control! I don't mean what I said."

Viggo jerks his chin in response as Wesley rejoins their little clique.

I've my own issue. Skirting the fire, I march towards Rowan and prepare to slam his mind with magic, too. But the white light from moments ago fills my head, again a blinding barrier.

"That was dumb, Violet," says Rowan when I manage to focus on him again. "Are you trying to incite trouble?"

"For Wesley? Just amusing myself." I straighten. "How dare you use a spell on me."

He laughs. "You forget that you're *half*-witch and I'm full-blooded. You may have superior skills once you add in the vamp half, but you're not me."

"And the vamp half is enough to warn you to keep away," I grit out. "I am not weaker than you."

He arches a brow. "Have I hit the Ice Queen's nerve? Weaker than you think, sweet Violet?"

This is worse than the time in the room that night he invaded—this time he hit first and my anger flared before I could catch hold of it. Does Rowan not understand what he's doing when he behaves like this?

I'm aware my heart beats faster, and not only from the magic that comes as a knee-jerk response to his actions. There's one major reason I avoid connecting with emotions—the energy I told Grayson that I'd never waste escapes when I do. If this triggers anger as an emotional response, there can be huge problems.

Anger and hatred fueled my father in his uncontrolled years, and I never joke when I say that I'm like him. Taking short, shallow breaths, I clench my fists, eyes closed, and fight against the emotion misting my mind.

"I suggest you step away," I say hoarsely. "Before you meet that vamp side."

"Your act doesn't work on—" He takes a sharp breath when I open my eyes again, the smirk wiped from his face by the vampire visage I've shifted to, my teeth sharper, eyes dark. "Shit," he mumbles and backs up.

His fear is enough to dampen down the growing anger and stop me from stepping forward and teasing him with threats. "Rowan Willowbrook. Do not attempt magic on me again. Ever."

But Dorian's dark part of me seizes on and loves that fear, so I close my eyes again as I desperately wrap a thick cover around the Blackwood part of the hybrid.

"And I have a bone to pick with you about runes painted on Wesley's floor!" No response. I open my eyes to continue and demand an answer, but he's gone.

I stare at the spot Rowan stood and swallow. I'm beginning to understand why my family kept me isolated from my peers, and why my father taught me to disengage whenever a strong feeling came over me. At the time, I believed he meant the urge to attack and kill. Now I understand he helped me bury more than urges.

Emotions.

They'd have the biggest effect on my behavior if uncontrolled, and I've just experienced why.

What kind of insanity led Dorian to send a teenage version of himself to Thornwood?

Chapter Sixteen

I REMAIN in the shadows where I stood with Rowan and survey the scene around me.

Is *this* what my life should be?

I've no desire to be accepted and liked amongst my peers, as I've no idea how I'd achieve that if I wanted to. But for the first time, I see the positive energy these people give each other.

Admittedly, a lot of alcohol and drug-fueled energy, but people *want* to be together. They *risk* negative outcomes. Is Grayson right? I need to learn more than just the language people speak? Such a ridiculous idea—why should I look at secret codes in people's bodies?

Rowan may've left, but I spy Leif who's now across the other side of the fire, holding a conversation with Viggo. I say 'conversation' but there's no doubt over *his* body language. Leif and the shifter are in each other's faces, almost nose to nose. My gaze flicks from person to person nearby. Several shifters stand close, paying little attention to the pair squaring up, while Wesley and his group have peeled themselves away from the masses and retreated to the edge of the woods.

Wesley seems to have forgotten my little magic trick, distracted by the girl now hanging onto his body and every word, gazing up at him as she clings to his waist. The girl who challenged me outside history class? Hard to tell from this distance when they're all so alike, but she's certainly proud of his attention.

Ugh.

Where did Rowan go? Planning something against me? I don't trust many people and definitely not him, especially now he's demonstrated he can match my witch skills.

Whatever the reason he met with Leif earlier, they're no longer together. Another argument or something else?

So much to discover and so much frustration. Time to leave.

I step from the solitary spot and walk back over to where Holly and Ollie sit on the ground in the same place. Not that I can speak to them, they're so engrossed in each other, emphasis on the *gross*. Blowing air into my cheeks, I wander to where I left my pink coat. Which is no longer on the ground. Frowning, I move around in case I'm looking in the wrong spot. Nothing. Why would somebody want such an item?

Surreptitiously, I look at the nearby groups for signs of the coat, but whoever took the item has either hidden it or left the gathering. Great. Holly won't be impressed, and she's one person I prefer to have on my side, mostly because she detracts attention from me. Her overwhelming exuberance creates a shiny barrier around my morose storm cloud personality, and despite my reservations early on, this makes her an excellent acquaintance.

A roar sounds across the campfire, and I snap my head round. Two people now tumble on the ground, exchanging blows as they roll around, each attempting to get the upper hand.

So much for the general tolerance between these factions.

Yet this is Leif and Viggo—which faction does *he* belong in?

I fold my arms across my chest and watch, intrigued by a physical fight. Most I've witnessed in the past involved magic.

"Shit." Holly appears beside me. "Is that Leif and Viggo?"

"Is this a common interaction between them?" I ask, still watching.

"Leif clashes with the shifters sometimes because he attends the academy and they don't like that," she explains. "Accuse him of believing he's superior to them."

"And is he?"

A small circle of kids from all three groups now surround the pair but don't interfere, shouting encouragement or watching warily, as if this is a planned boxing match. The viciousness of the punches Leif throws matches his opponent, and I wince at the sound of bone cracking. If this were a planned match, a referee is sorely needed.

"I don't get involved with the shifters," says Holly. "Some cause trouble."

"As I can see."

Wesley shoves his way through the gathered spectators and snatches the back of Leif's jacket, who turns to look at him and is rewarded with a fist to the face. Leif stumbles back and falls close to where Viggo's on the ground.

Curiously, Wesley and Viggo don't continue their assault on Leif, who scrambles to his hands and knees before springing to his feet and sprinting into the woods. Wesley looks down at the shifter and nods, extending a hand to help him. The shifter ignores the hand and deftly jumps up. These kids may not be full shifters yet, but they already have traits. He's as big as Wesley, but broader shouldered, forearms thick and knotted. Bear?

Then what's Leif? He managed to get the upper hand over a bear shifter who're known for their superior strength, and he moved quickly when he ran. Not a wolf. A big cat of some kind? Shifters range from four-legged mammals to birds, and also the occasional and rare dragon. The dragons aren't part of any society but rule their own kind and live underground. Not literally—there's a mafia or two run by dragons.

Weirder still, the shifter steps up to Wesley and jabs a finger into his chest. As Wesley squares up, Holly groans. "I think Wes's comment upset Viggo."

"Oh."

"You triggered this, Violet. You wanted Wes hurt." Holly's voice is hushed, an edge of disgust in the tone.

Do I really need this conversation again? "No. I'm ambivalent regarding Wesley's physical safety."

Ollie gives me a 'huh?' look, then slides his eyes to Holly. "Violet means she doesn't care what happens to him."

"I'm glad somebody understands what she says. No offence, Violet, but you speak with odd words." Ollie offers a smile. "Call me simple for not understanding them all."

"Very well. But don't feel bad. You're unable to help your inferior capacity for learning."

"Violet..." Again, Holly sighs, then nods in the direction of the confrontation. "At least somebody is interfering."

Wesley's girl is by his side, tugging at her boyfriend's sleeve and whispering something in his ear. His shoulders drop and he shrugs away her hand before storming back to his group. She scurries after him and again tries to get Wesley's attention.

Wesley grabs a bottle of alcohol from one of his friends and stomps away into the dark—in Leif's direction. His crestfallen girlfriend watches him go.

I'm intrigued that Wesley's gang paid zero attention to the fight and still act as if nothing around has happened—not one person moved from their place or paused the conversation.

"Hey, Viggo! Not such a big guy now, huh?" somebody shouts. Kai steps forward and crosses his arms, looking at the shifter, and all voices hush. "You were losing against the academy kid."

"Fuck you," shouts back Viggo. "Unless you want me to kick the crap out of you, too."

Laughter from the humans accompanies a snort from Kai. "Wouldn't be a good idea, my friend." Viggo lurches forward, but two of his gang stop him, holding arms behind his back, talking urgently.

"I'll fuck you *both* up!" snarls Viggo. "Starting with you."

"Go ahead," jeers Kai. "That'll be the opportunity everybody is waiting for. We can show the town what the shifters are—vicious, bullying assholes."

"Watch your fucking mouth."

"We should leave before things kick off," mutters Ollie. "I don't want to be caught up in this if authorities end up involved."

Holly narrows her eyes at me. "Did you have anything to do with Wes's behavior?" I blink and say nothing. "Violet..."

I chew my lip. Fascinating as this tableau of teenage life is, I'm done here. "I agree. Let's leave. I'm bored now."

But Holly's gaze remains trained on the shifter and human. "Someone needs to stop them. Can't you use your magic again?"

"I'm not the only witch here that can use mental magic," I retort. "And it appears *they* don't want to get involved. Neither do I. Let the silly boys play their games."

"Holly." Ollie jerks his head towards a spot a few feet away from us. "Can we talk?"

"Uh. Okay." She nods at me. "Wait there, Violet."

"I need to find your coat," I announce, and turn away. "I'll meet you back at the academy."

"You lost my *coat*?" she shrieks after me, as I head off. *That's* what bothers her the most about this evening? "I'm waiting here for you! Don't go far!"

Skirting around the outliers, I head in the direction Leif and Wesley ran. Is Wesley following him? Rowan may rejoin Leif too, and I've yet to figure out what they're planning.

Because on some level, this involves me. Why else would the asshole break into my room and try to steal something?

SHIFTERS ARE THE EASIEST OF CREATURES TO SCENT, BUT I struggle to pick up Leif's, as if his stealth ability extends to his animal pheromones. I can't detect Rowan either, and I'm learning to pick up on the tang to his aura along with the energy pulse from his magic.

Hmm.

These woods are denser than I expected with low brambles that scratch at Holly's cutesy leggings. I pause and lift my face, inhaling as I sharpen my sight and hearing. There're small rodents scurrying and sleeping birds in the trees, but nothing else.

Not even a pink coat.

A shape streaks by me, winding through the trees.

A vampire. Why? They don't attend the human and shifter Friday rituals.

Within a heartbeat or two, I catch the figure and spin in front until he almost hits me.

"Grayson?"

There's no smile or clever comment this time as he stares back, arms loosely by his side. Blood streaks Grayson's face, but frustratingly my senses are dulled against whether this is human, witch, or shifter. A breath rushes from me. "What did—"

I'm too stunned to follow as he blends back into the woods, a shadow moving faster than moments ago. Grayson's and the blood's indistinct scent tracks back in the direction of the gathering and I hurry along, following where he traveled across the leaf-strewn ground and barely left an imprint.

I pick up another faint scent from a nearby tree, and that joins with Grayson's and the blood. Running my fingers along the rough bark, I then lift them to my nose. The scent is vague but one that immediately evokes images of Leif the day in the classroom. Earthy, barely detectable over the mossy scent from the bark.

Then Grayson's scent stops.

I straighten as a thought hits me. Did Grayson attack Leif? Why would he do that?

I'm too intrigued to turn away now and creep rather than run, focusing on any more blood scent to join that of Leif, frustrated again that my mother's potion dulls my ability. But the blood scent trail also stopped.

As I hear voices, I'm happy that I snuck rather than surged onwards. Leif and Rowan's voices become clearer as I advance on them, but still too low for me to hear the conversation. Between two trees, Leif's sitting on the ground, head in his hands as Rowan crouches in front of him and talks quickly.

If Leif is conscious, and Rowan is with him, Grayson didn't attack. I don't need to interfere. Yet a doubt niggles— Leif ran from the fire and now he looks worse.

Still, not my problem if he's alive.

As I turn and make my way back to the fire and waiting Holly, I'm confused. Not because I don't understand why blood covered Grayson's face, but that the sight prompted me to search for his victim.

What sent me chasing through the woods after the trail left by Grayson? An innate desire to find the bleeding victim or one of concern for the person?

Other people aren't my concern. So why? A disturbing thought hits.

Did the blood on Grayson's face tempt a hidden part of me?

Chapter Seventeen

HOLLY HOLDS the coat hanger in front of her face, and I don't need to know body language to be aware what her sigh means.

"I'm sorry you lost your coat," I say as I lace up my black brogues. After last night's wardrobe choice, I'm not complaining about the uniform.

"*You* lost my coat." Her eyes remain on the empty hanger.

"Somebody must've taken it. Watch out for someone wearing the coat. It's distinctive." I smile in what I hope is an encouraging way. "I understand if you never want to lend me any clothes again."

Hopefully.

With a humph, Holly replaces the hanger then studies me, brow creased. "You haven't wanted to attend breakfast before. Why the sudden desire to visit the cafeteria?"

I shrug. "Perhaps the experience last night encouraged me to become more sociable."

"How? You only spoke to Rowan and Wes. What *did* you speak to Rowan about?" She retrieves her own shoes from under the bed. "Is he the 'opportunity' you mentioned?"

"Is there a reason that you see all my student interaction as a romantic entanglement?" I ask tersely.

"I'm teasing. Can't you tell?"

"No." I watch as she picks up her phone, immediately distracted by the screen, then furiously begins tapping, chewing her lip. "If I bought one of those, would people contact me?" I ask.

She looks up. "Yes. That's the point of owning a phone."

"But *constantly*? And yours never rings. Isn't that what a phone is supposed to do?"

"Oh, no. *Nobody* phones. Everybody sends texts." She waves the phone at me.

"And you say *I'm* odd."

"Why are you asking? Were you thinking of getting a phone?" She perks up. "That would be awesome, you could keep in touch with everything happening at Thornwood."

I stare. "No. I only want the camera."

"Then buy a camera."

Ignoring her, I tap my foot. "But if nobody has my number, I'm safe from anybody sending me inane messages?"

"Yes."

"Even you?"

Holly's lips go thin. "If you refuse to give me your number, yes. I won't send you *inane messages*." She's terse. Have I upset her again? "But you should have an emergency contact."

"For what?"

"Emergencies."

"I don't have emergencies. That suggests I'm incapable of solving issues."

"You're not immune to *everything*, Violet." She tips her head. "Or are you?"

"Good question." I stand and take hold of my bag. "But I can protect myself."

Standing, Holly pushes her phone into her bag of textbooks. "I'll take you to buy a phone if you like?"

"In town?" She smiles and nods. "In a *mall*?"

Hmm. Maybe I'll manage with a pen and paper.

———

THE REASON I WANT TO SUBJECT MYSELF TO BREAKFAST WITH the masses? Because I want to spy—who's there, who isn't, who talks to who. I spent some time considering what caused my behavior last night and came to a further conclusion.

I like to be in control of my environment and if people are acting in a way that disrupts the status quo, I must take action to remedy the situation as I don't appreciate that disruption.

Especially witches who seem to think they can invade my space *and* my mind.

Thankfully, there's enough room for the dining area to hold the majority of the academy, including the students in different years, all seated around round tables placed close together. The dark wood and tiled floor aesthetic extends to the cafeteria, quite the opposite to the easy-clean tables and chairs from the high school.

As I walk through the door, I side-step to stand against the wall and Holly pauses beside me. I'm immediately disappointed that none of the three guys are in the room and available for me to spy on. Although I'm more than happy that Wesley isn't here.

"Should we sit—" A familiar girl strides towards us and cuts Holly's words dead as she shoves my roommate out of the way.

"Kirsten!" protests Holly.

Why are her cheeks pink? There's sun shining through the large windows, but the room isn't particularly hot.

"Where is he?" Kirsten shouts in my face.

"Which he are you referring to? I don't know the location of many males," I reply.

"Wesley. He never returned to the academy last night."

Her gaze remains steady on my face as she attempts to read me; I read her mind. All I see is a tangled mess of anger and upset, so I retreat.

"Why would I know his whereabouts?" I ask.

"Kirsten, Wes sometimes stays out all night on a Friday," says Holly gently.

"Yes. But he always answers his phone for *me*," she retorts.

"Holly told me nobody answers their phone," I say. "Therefore, why would he?"

"Violet, I was half-joking. I mean, we don't *usually*."

I flash her a look. "Your jokes are hard to identify."

Kirsten's cheeks fire redder, and she swears at me before balling her fists at her side. "Everybody heard you threaten him."

"They did?" I ask, and raise my voice. "Do you mean all the people currently staring at me rather than eating?"

"Well, Wes asked if you were threatening him," she corrects, and I sigh. "Then you followed him!"

"I was looking for Leif."

"Maybe Wes passed out drunk?" suggests Holly. "It's early yet. He'll be back. Seems unfair to immediately accuse Violet of harming him."

"He isn't answering his phone!" Kirsten's voice rises. "If I call Wes, he *always* picks up."

"Kirsten, perhaps Wesley didn't answer because he's with another girl and doesn't want you to know?" I suggest.

"Violet," mutters Holly and nudges me.

Ugh. The signs are there—this girl is edging towards mild hysteria that's aimed at me. I've experienced this a few times in a school setting. "I'm sure nothing serious has befallen him."

"Nothing *serious*? So, something has? What did you do?" she bats back.

Good grief. I turn to Holly. "I've changed my mind about breakfast."

"Ha! You *are* scared to answer questions." Kirsten's voice continues to rise in pitch. "You hate him! We knew you were waiting for a chance to strike."

"You are a ridiculous girl," I say calmly. "I don't hate anybody, and I don't 'strike'. If you look around the school, you may find others who *do*. Please settle down."

Her mouth flaps open and closed as the poor thing struggles for words.

"Holly. Could you get me a coffee and one of those squishy cakes?" I ask.

"Muffins. Remind me how you have your coffee?"

"In a tall paper cup." I point at a young girl sipping from one as she watches us with gleeful amusement.

"Yes. But do you want milk or not?"

"Ah. I have my coffee black." I smirk at Kirsten. "To match my soul."

I'M NOT INTERESTED IN COFFEE OR MUFFINS AND WALK straight from the main building to the wing that holds Sheridan House—the vampires. I don't know which room Grayson lives in, nor if he's there, so I loiter at the bottom of the wide staircase. He wasn't in the cafeteria, and I doubt he's the type to head to class early.

My patience is rewarded when he appears at the top—I knew he'd be one of the last to leave. Grayson's in uniform, his dark hair pulled neatly back, face no longer smeared with blood.

And immediately senses me.

He pulls on his bottom lip as he regards me before reaching the bottom of the stairs and shooting off to his left.

Well, the fact Grayson is avoiding me adds to the intrigue.

I stride after him, readying myself to up my speed when I turn a corner and spot him again with a teacher. Grayson's eyes dart between me and the man, nodding in agreement to the teacher's reprimand. Then Grayson dashes off again, and the teacher continues walking until he reaches me. I've never met him, but his aura and cheekbones tell me this guy is a vamp.

The teacher nods and shining dark hair strokes his shoulders. "Do I need to remind you of academy rules, too?" he asks tersely.

"Is there a list? How many do I need to break before I'm removed from campus?" The man peers at me as many do, attempting to judge if I'm serious. What did Grayson do?

"Running at high speeds is forbidden. Collisions between vampires and humans often end in concussions."

I blow air into my cheeks, one eye on Grayson's disappearing figure. "I strive to avoid physical contact with people, so you needn't worry."

And I need to move before Grayson evades me. The teacher allows me to go, and I grit my teeth as I hold back running faster, the teacher's scrutiny almost tangible as I hurry along.

Grayson isn't moving at the speed he was but still an unnatural one. As he walks through the building exit, I take a quick look around me before catching up to him. As with last night, I circle around so he's facing me and has to stop.

"Good morning, Grayson," I say.

His green eyes are as impassive as the rest of his expression. "Good morning, Violet."

"How was your evening?" I continue.

"A curious question from the girl who doesn't think of me because I'm irrelevant." Grayson steps backwards before walking by.

"You're relevant to me currently." He scoffs quietly and keeps walking. Taking a sharp breath, I stride after the vampire. "I have a question." No response. "Whose blood did I see on your face?"

Grayson stops dead. "At the graveyard? I didn't have blood on my face."

"No. Later. In the woods." The moment his eyes meet mine, I send out a wave of magic but fail to enter his mind. Vamps are superior mental magic users and Grayson's definitely well-versed in constructing a barrier.

"Mind reading is rude, Violet. Or is that the only way you can understand people?" His voice remains flat, and he remains detached from me. "I imagine you'll enjoy the mental magic classes."

"Whose blood did I see on your face?" I repeat.

Again, he's shuttered, unblinking. "Am I so relevant that you *dream* of me, Violet? Because you haven't *seen* me with blood on my face."

I close the gap between us as something tickles at my mental shield. "I suggest you don't attempt to influence *my* thoughts, Grayson. Did you change somebody's memories of your attack with those oh-so-mesmerizing eyes? Or is your victim dead?"

"I did not attack anybody."

"Not Wesley?"

"He wasn't on campus last night, so I had no need to interfere with his bullying once I returned after seeing you."

"And Wesley *still* isn't on campus. A whiny human girl

accused me of hurting him. She seemed rather concerned that something happened because he's unable to use his phone."

"Why are you staring at me like that?" Grayson leans down until our faces are almost level. "You can't read body language and can't see into my mind. Are you waiting for a confession?"

"What about Leif? Did you hurt him?" I continue.

He sighs. "No. I didn't speak to him or Rowan."

Interesting. "How do you know Rowan was with Leif? They don't hang out much. You *were* in the woods."

Grayson sucks his lips together. "I'm busy, Violet."

"You're evasive, Grayson. I know what I saw."

We stand off beneath the gray sky, two figures between the academy building and the cloisters, as if waiting for the rain. I relish the cool breeze that blows against my cheeks, and even if it rained, we could stand here for hours, neither feeling the cold. Why doesn't Grayson tell me the truth instead of this pretense?

"I'm not interested in speaking to you." Grayson gives me a long look, then turns back to the building and walks away.

His words strike me. Neither am I, usually, yet here I am chasing someone through the academy. Chasing Grayson.

Chapter Eighteen

CLASSES ON A SATURDAY. What fresh Hell is this place? The academy names Potions class 'Chemistry class', presumably so those with zero magic ability can still join in and make pretty colored liquids. Sometimes, the supes study old texts that teach established and simple concoctions, while the humans peruse textbooks to assist them in passing the human exams. Other times, all work on potions that humans have little success in creating. Today, the humans assist the supes.

Witches and vamps need to reach an expected level of proficiency in many lessons but don't face exams unless they want to attend a human university. That's a path the supes can take if they're inclined, but most here can ascend to good positions in society just by attending Thornwood.

I've never considered my future, but a nice, solitary research position appeals to me. There's much to be learned about necromancy, and the benefits rather than hysteria. After all, only a few are born with the ability, and shouldn't we utilize such a unique magic?

I haven't reanimated anything since the mice, and I have a conundrum—I hate animal cruelty but would need a freshly deceased creature to practice with. Otherwise, I'd be no better than those who killed the mice. I'm on the lookout for opportunities even though I've agreed not to practice without my mother present, but I don't see the problem if it's animals. Reanimating a human could be beyond my capabilities, anyway. But that's a goal.

Everybody needs something to strive for in life. Or death.

The tall stools face benches covered in apparatus for distilling and mixing, ingredients kept in a cupboard behind the witch teaching us. Since handing out small amounts of liquids and powders, Mr. Woodside locked the cupboard. He's a younger witch than most teachers, but his sour face and soul-piercing eyes assist him in keeping his class under control.

I'm beside my loyal friend who's refusing to elaborate what's in the whispers about Wesley, not that there's much doubt: Violet's involved in Wesley's alleged disappearance. Rowan sits a few rows behind me so I can't watch him, and Grayson hasn't attended. Leif is missing, but nobody mentions him.

"Has the bully not returned yet?" I ask casually as I spoon ground amethyst into a small vial.

Holly steadies the rack holding the vials. "Wesley? No. His father's worried now, too. A few students at the fire last night were called to his office."

"Not me? How unusual," I comment.

An acrid smell hits me when I uncork the bottle of sulphur and take hold of a pipette. Years of boredom as a child makes me an adept potion maker and eight-year-old me could concoct this potion many struggle with now.

"I'm sure the school *will* talk to you. And me." Holly hands me a small metal spoon and as I stir the liquid and powder, they blend into a deep green. "You're good at this. Normally, we take ages to create potions this color." She holds up a strip of paper that indicates that we've matched the necessary color to complete our task.

"Are we allowed to leave now?" I ask Holly and push the stool back in anticipation.

"Not until the lesson ends."

"What?" I complain and sit, elbows on the bench and both hands beneath my chin. "That's a long time."

"Thirty minutes, Violet. Here. You can help me learn my formulas while we wait." As she pulls a human textbook out of her bag, I huff and rest my cheek on the bench.

Mr. Woodside watches us before returning to reading a book. Hardly what I call tuition. The glaring from other kids scrapes at my nerves, not because I care what the students think, but because the bad energy gives me a headache. I wander through a couple of their minds and see the same thing: *the freak attacked Wesley, what if he's dead?*

A group of vamps and humans are more interested in talking than finishing their half-hearted attempts at the lesson. I've seen them together several times—some of the few who mingle between the races. I'm under their scrutiny as much as the other students, and I'm on the verge of leaving.

One vamp guy and girl appear particularly close. The blond-haired vamp reminds me a little of Dorian, since few have the coloring, and the girl was in the lunch group when Holly introduced me to the academy. Name? No idea.

The slender girl stands and glances at the teacher. "I need more sulphur. We ran out." She points at the container on our bench. "They have some spare."

Mr. Woodside nods and as she edges towards us, the vamp sits straight, eyes shining with… something.

"That's okay, isn't it?" she asks Holly and reaches out for the bottle. A drop of blood hits the bench, and she lifts her hand to her face. "Oh!"

Her surprise couldn't be any faker. "You appear to have cut yourself," I say evenly.

She bites her lip. "I'm not sure how. Paper cut?"

I snort and nod at the blond vamp. "His teeth."

Holly remains silent as the girl cradles her hand against her chest. Whatever cut her skin must be deep, since the blood slides along her fingers and covers her hand.

"I hope I'm not *bothering* you," she says sweetly.

"Not at all. You have one uninjured hand. Take the bottle with that," I inform her.

I dutifully took my 'don't butcher humans' medicine this morning and can barely scent the blood, nor is there any appeal. What is the point in this girl's ridiculous behavior? I fix a hard stare on the blond vamp who merely smirks.

Something thuds on the floor beside me, and the girl's self-satisfied expression drops away. I turn my head to where she's staring.

Holly, unconscious beside her stool on the hard tiles, face drained of blood.

Good grief.

"Has she hurt herself?" The girl's voice rises in panic as she moves around the bench towards Holly.

"Holly faints at the sight of blood. That's your fault. Keep away." Isabella says, and she's off her stool and over to us in the blink of an eye, crouching beside Holly, with a palm on the unconscious girl's cheek.

"What on earth is happening?" Mr. Woodside finally interacts with his students as he rises and moves over. "Why is Holly on the floor?"

Holly groans and opens her eyes before turning onto her side and mumbling apologies. *Apologies?* To *who*?

"Somebody help the girl up," he says crossly, then catches sight of the culprit. "What happened to your hand, Laura?"

"Quite evidently, Laura cut herself." I shove back the

stool, an escape route from class firmly in my sights. "I'll take Holly to the nurse. She needs a cup of water."

That's what Holly needed last time; I'm unsure what water contains that cures fainting in humans, but it appears necessary.

"Did you hit your head?" Mr. Woodside asks Holly, and she mumbles 'no'. "Violet. Take Holly outside the classroom and sit on a bench until she's well enough to walk to the nurse." The teacher shakes his head. "No. Isabella. You take her. Laura. Clean yourself up." He shoots a look at the vamp guy, who pulls an innocent look. "If the blood was for *you*, there'll be consequences. No taking blood from humans on campus."

"I believe the blood was for me," I say, and Mr. Woodside's mouth drops open. "To *provoke* me. Unfortunately, all they provoked was Holly's phobia."

"I'm okay," she mumbles.

"You don't look okay," I say as Isabella helps her stand.

"I'll take her," says Isabella.

"No. I insist. Can you walk, Holly?" I take hold of her bag and the wobbly-legged girl nods at me.

We're barely a step out of the classroom door before Holly collapses in my arms again. I hold the heavy girl upright and stare at her curly head, totally lost what to do. I've never experienced weakness like this in acquaintances before.

With a sigh, I hoist her over my shoulder and begin my quest for a cup of water.

Chapter Nineteen

CARRYING fellow students in a fireman's lift can't be common because the nurse greets me with stunned surprise when I knock on the infirmary door. She's human, but do they have witch and vampire medical staff at the academy? A lamia vamp would help with calming down distressed patients. Hemia vamps? Not such a smart idea.

The gray-haired human woman rushes me inside to a waiting bed, which I try to lie Holly on but partially dropped her.

This does the trick in waking Holly.

"I'm sorry," Holly mumbles again as the nurse tucks a pillow beneath her head.

"I'm confused why you apologize for something out of your control. Your unconsciousness had no effect on anybody," I say as the nurse walks away for water.

Holly looks up at me, deathly pale, and perspiring, but I can hear her sluggish heartbeat beginning to return to normal. "I'm embarrassed."

And still making no sense.

The nurse returns with the necessary drink and gently

props Holly to take sips. I watch Holly; how awful to be affected by something so minor and nonsensical.

"This is your second faint in a few days," comments the nurse as she takes Holly's wrist. "Perhaps we should draw some blood and check a few things. Your iron could be low."

Holly's newly returned pink pales again. "I'm fine."

"Clearly you're not," I reply.

The nurse pats Holly's hand. "We do get students with low iron who need treatment. Are you in a relationship with a vampire?" I snort out a laugh and the nurse frowns at me. "This is an issue within the academy. Even though there's no intention of damage, taking blood has consequences for those who like to experiment."

"I don't," says Holly as she sips the water. "And I never could if blood makes me pass out."

Human students experimenting with fledgling hemia vampires? That could result in a worse outcome than low iron. And if witches join in then they're crazy—witch blood can send even the most controlled vampire out of that control.

"I'll find you an iron tonic, anyway. Girls your age often need supplements even without..." She trails off and gives a tight smile. "Rest. I'll be back in a few."

There's a hard wooden chair beside the bed, and I sit. "Humans are more deficient than I realized."

"But everybody has their weaknesses, Violet." She leans across the bed to place the half-empty paper cup on the tall nightstand.

"I don't."

"You'll have one."

"Mmm." I blow air into my cheeks and peruse the rest of the room. Beside Holly's bed, there're two opposite and one beside her. The one facing us has pale blue curtains drawn around. Brightly lit by large windows, the place smells like lavender and peppermint, but despite the coziness, the room's sterility and cleanliness make this a place few would want to stay for long.

"You were kind to help me, thank you," says Holly.

I look back. "No need to thank me. I wanted to leave class; you offered me the opportunity."

"Oh." Holly's mouth turns down. "Well, I'm glad I was useful."

"Yes. Me too. Thank you."

She doesn't reply. Conversation must be difficult after such trauma.

Soft footsteps cross the tiles, and the nurse reappears with two tiny paper cups, then slips behind the thin blue curtain.

"Take these every six hours. They'll help with the pain." A male voice mumbles something. "We're now happy that there's no concussion, Leif, so yes, you'll be able to leave in an hour."

My eyes go wide, and I strain my hearing, but they barely exchange any more words. *Pain. Concussion.*

The door to the infirmary bangs open and closed, and the nurse emerges from the curtain, hurrying out to attend to the new arrival. "My, we're having a busy day."

"No Wesley?" I ask.

She pauses and turns back. "Why do you ask?"

"I heard he was missing. Thought he might be here."

The nurse stares at me for a few moments longer, then hurries away.

Holly lies beneath a white blanket, eyes closed, so I take my opportunity. As I sidle through the gap in the curtains, Leif yanks a sheet across his broad, naked chest, staring at me from where he sits in the bed.

"What are you doing here?" he snaps.

"Would you believe me if I told you I'm a concerned friend?"

"No. I would not."

I slant my head. "Why are you covering your chest like that? I'm not about to tear your heart out."

He blinks at me, then shakes his head. "Can you pass my T-shirt?"

The clothing on the chair matches the scent from the woods last night and the gray T-shirt I hand to him is streaked with blood and dirt. As he pulls the item over his head, Leif reveals scratch marks and bruises on his chest to match those yellowing on his face.

"Aren't you bothered that they're treating you like a human?" I ask. "A shifter wouldn't suffer a concussion or need pain killers. Your bruises are already healing."

He touches the mark on his cheek. "I *asked* to stay to avoid questions when I return to class. My injuries won't be obvious soon."

"Everybody will ask questions about why you fought with Viggo. That was rather public. Why did you?"

"He threw the first punch," retorts Leif.

"Because...?"

"Because he's a dick." Leif clamps his mouth shut as I watch expectantly. "That's it. Nothing more to say."

After placing the other clothes from the chair onto the bed, I sit, and he scowls. Grayson accuses me of not reading body language, but there're a few things I've seen enough to recognize as normal responses to me: scowling, disbelief, and on occasion, disgust. Although to be honest, that's normally vocalized too.

"Did Wesley find you in the woods after you walked away from the fight?" I continue.

"No," he says sharply.

"Only Rowan? I saw you in the woods with him."

"There were a few people at the fire last night."

"No. *In* the woods, not at the edge. You were hurt and Rowan was with you. What happened?"

Leif snorts at me. "You just said—I fought with Viggo."

"Yes. But when you left, why not head back to the academy? You went deeper into the woods and met Rowan. Why?" I press.

"And that's your business *why*?" he asks.

"Did Grayson attack you after you left the fire?" I ask and gesture at his chest. "They looked like different scratches to a shifter's. Or are your injuries from a fight with Wesley after fighting Viggo?"

Curtain rings sound against metal as the nurse pulls back the curtain. "Violet. You need to leave."

Only now am I aware of the loud sobbing from the direction of the entry, a girl's voice bordering on wailing.

"Violet," says the nurse, and I jerk away as she takes my arm. "Leave."

A girl walks towards the bed beside Holly's, barely able to move without assistance from the concerned man holding her up. Long hair falls across her face as she bends over back heaving, but as the nurse says my name the third time, she looks up.

Kirsten. She's as pale as Holly currently is, but with splotchy red cheeks, and her glazed eyes meet mine. The anguish radiating from her is matched by the hatred sharing that energy.

"You," she chokes out. "It was you! I found him!"

I barely need to touch Kirsten's mind to find the memory that takes up every inch of space right now.

Wesley. Sprawled on the ground in the woods, dead eyes and throat ripped open. His limbs are twisted at unnatural angles and his chest... *His chest.* In the center, above his heart, a rune.

A Blackwood rune.

Chapter Twenty

I KNEW my parents would return, but not within the hour.

Dorian's Blackwood blood runes help the pair travel; the runes certainly haven't helped me with anything apart from a false accusation.

He's with me now in the headteachers' office, my mother in the other seat, the pair either side of their daughter. Eloise sits upright but Dorian lounges backwards, legs stretched forward as he regards the headteachers.

"If Violet says she never killed the boy, that's the truth. There's nothing else to say here," he says simply.

Mr. Willis swings between purple-faced anger and wan-faced distress as my parents subtly use their mental magic on him. But his emotions are too violent and unpredictable to get a handle on. Understandably, as he's lost a child.

"The *rune*?" he barks.

"I've seen the photograph from the scene." Dorian pulls a disgusted face. "A badly drawn Blackwood rune. Violet learned to etch them *precisely* while very young."

"With respect," says Eloise. "If Violet killed your son, leaving a rune would leave evidence."

"*Unless* she destroyed his body afterwards," Mr. Willis snaps back. "That poor girl discovered Wesley close to a fire and we believe the killer was disturbed before he or she could throw my son's body *onto* that fire."

"Well, this person sounds like a sloppy killer," I comment, and my mother takes a sharp breath as Mr. Willis slams his hands on the desk, shoving back his chair to stand. Oh. Whoops. "I meant, you're looking for someone who *doesn't* contain a natural strength or ability to dispose of a body." The poisonous look continues. "I did not murder Wesley; I would've finished the job and not left him by the fire."

"What?" shouts Mr. Willis and lunges forward.

Dorian moves to stand between me and Mr. Willis while Eloise hisses at me to stop talking. "If I'm accused, I have to defend myself!" I protest. "And this is the truth. I—"

"*I* don't think you should say anymore," says Eloise softly. "This is a highly charged, emotional situation for all of us."

"Not for me or Dad," I mutter under my breath.

"Violet is our main suspect," says Mrs. Lorcan. "There's no avoiding that."

"There were more than a dozen kids present last night," I protest. "Question *them*."

"We intend to, once authorities arrive and begin the investigation," she continues.

"Human *and* supernatural," puts in Mr. Willis and sits. "This happened on land under human jurisdiction. *That*, Mr. Blackwood, means that you do not have full authority over the investigation or the outcome."

The resulting silence might be familiar to me but isn't to the two headteachers. Dorian takes a step forward and presses his hands on the desk, the only thing between him and Mr. Willis. I can picture how his face has transformed, not vampiric, but some*thing* with a malevolent edge.

"My daughter did not kill your son. She will remain at the academy and co-operate fully with any investigation. When Violet's name is cleared, I expect a personal apology from you, *Mr. Willis*." Dorian's growl even sends a shiver through me.

"Dorian." My mother approaches and touches his hand. My father's aggression won't help my cause, only paint a darker picture of my family.

Knowing Dorian's violent history, I'm constantly surprised that he keeps the leadership role he does. At my age, he'd likely have killed, not consulted with, a human. Of course, my mother Eloise softened the black-hearted hybrid, the love of a good woman and all that, but his history is never mentioned to the humans.

They'd be less than accepting of him and certainly wouldn't understand why somebody with Dorian's power is *needed* to oversee our society. He invokes a dread awe that's enough to keep all supes in line.

But that's not what bothers me the most. "Dorian, why don't you agree I should leave now?" I ask.

He slowly turns, blinking until his coal-black eyes become their captivating blue again. "And indicate we're trying to hide you from so-called justice? No, sweetest girl."

My teeth clench hard as I bite back a retort; a plea.

"*If* you can guarantee Violet's safety," puts in my mother, looking between Dorian and Mrs. Lorcan.

"No special treatment for Violet," snaps the purple-faced headmaster.

"I don't expect or desire that. If I must stay."

"Others might want to end their associations with you," says Mrs. Lorcan softly.

"Oh *no*," I say with heavy sarcasm and hold a hand on my heart. "All the wonderful friends I've made?"

"I'm talking about Holly," says Mrs. Lorcan. "We may

need to change who you room with. Removing you from Darwin House may be wise, too."

"No." Dorian's tone is firm and terse. "I won't allow you to do anything that even *slightly* hints at Violet's involvement. Her life here continues as normal."

What does Dorian count as normal?

Chapter Twenty-One

I'm unsurprised when Dorian rushes off straight after our parent-teacher interview; a human death at a supes hand takes special handling. With his daughter implicated, Dorian will need to cajole, threaten, or subdue his subordinates into keeping an open mind while the investigation continues.

Dorian wants and needs to be the first from the supernatural government to meet with the town's authorities to discuss the way forward.

Eloise is hesitant about leaving me, but she shares my concern over Dorian's next move. His anger flaring at Mr. Willis only heralds what might come next, and Dorian needs her calming presence much more than I do.

The pair alerted my other two fathers, Ethan and Zeke, who are traveling down in order for us to meet as a family and more thoroughly discuss events. Before today, I would've begged the pair to take me from Thornwood, but the more I consider this, the greater the realization that now I *can't* leave.

Not until I figure out who killed Wesley—and why. Sure, he was a violent and unpleasant person, but for someone to go as far as *murder*... Until I clear my name, I'll be in a blinding spotlight and unable to hide in the shadows of student society. And until I know *why*, others could be in danger.

Once my parents leave, I turn back to the academy building. Last time, when they left me staring at my new gray-bricked home, I seethed with resentment. Now, the place offers me something new. In this case, the enemy of my enemy was *not* a friend, and is attempting to frame me for murder. I'm not only clearing my name, but I've something to fill the mundane hours. Discover who.

Finally, something interesting to put my mind to.

The game is on.

I return to Darwin House's building, fully expecting repercussions from those who've thrown accusations my way. News must've spread by now—Leif heard Kirsten's outburst and if he's discharged from the infirmary, he'll at least tell Rowan.

But the building contains nothing but quiet—and the mingled smell of human perspiration, perfumes, and deodorants that hang in the air. No students. Not one.

Weird. But useful.

Inside my room, I pull out a black pen and large notepad, then begin to write a timeline from yesterday evening. Notes on conversations I've heard. Interactions I've seen. Chewing my lip, I also study the words I found inside the book. Before Eloise left, I asked if she recognized the language, but she didn't. Her ancestry's as old as the Blackwoods, if she hasn't encountered this before, the text could be ancient or not witch-based at all.

I *swear* Rowan wrote this.

I'm missing a lot of information—most notably the full condition of Wesley's body and method of murder. I need a clearer view than the snapshot in Kirsten's mind.

Snapshot.

How do I get hold of the photos, or get closer to the investigation? As the main suspect, authorities are hardly likely to invite me to participate unless it's a confession.

Arms crossed over my chest, I slump back in the chair and scowl at the blank spaces on the paper as if they deliberately taunt me, unaware that Holly is in the room until she speaks.

"Are you alright, Violet?"

I look over. She's lost her pallor and replaced the academy uniform with jeans and a black jumper, her expression as subdued as her clothing.

"No. I am not alright."

"Because you're accused of killing Wes?" she asks and approaches me.

I spot the outstretched hand, ready to give me comfort, and narrow my eyes until she tucks both beneath her arms instead. "No. I'm annoyed because I need more clues and information."

"You're not worried something will happen?"

"To me?" I shrug. "Dorian won't allow any action against me without hard evidence."

"I mean, the other students might retaliate."

"Oh. Them? No." I turn in my seat. "Who do you think killed him?" Holly bites her lip. "Me?"

"I *think* you'll struggle to find the answer alone." She looks over my shoulder at the notes. "And outsiders at the academy don't usually get help."

"You're all stupid," I announce and snap the notebook closed. "If I'm the investigation's focus, the authorities will miss the real killer. That person could strike again."

"Not if the crime was personal, Violet, and everybody thinks it was." She sinks onto her bed and takes hold of a plush pig, pulling at its ears. "Everybody heard Wes accuse you of threatening him."

"The bully has other enemies."

"He has for years. But people see it as a coincidence that he dies shortly after you arrived." Holly squishes the pig to her chest. "I'm not saying *I* believe that, but—"

"Did you know Grayson plays vigilante?" I interrupt.

She blinks. "Yes, but he wasn't at the gathering last night."

"Wasn't he? I saw him in the graveyard, remember?"

And the woods. But I'm not sharing all my information with Holly yet.

"Vamps don't go near fire. Wes's body was found near a fire."

"Hmm." I flip open the notebook and scrawl beneath his name: 'fire??' "Not proof. How about Leif? He was in the infirmary with worse injuries than Viggo inflicted. A fight to the death?"

"Leif?" She frowns. "He fights with shifters but not usually Wes. They ignore each other—Leif's too big for Wes to bully."

I nod and write a note.

"What are you doing?" she asks and stands again.

"Clearing my name. Any other suspects? Other humans or vamps? Witches?" I tap the pen against my teeth. "Rowan?"

She stares at me as if I'm insane. "Rowan and Wes ignore each other."

"As far as you *know*."

"Wes picks on weak kids. He tried to bully Rowan once and discovered why he shouldn't. Rowan's a skilled witch." As *I* know.

"What happened?"

She shrugs. "Nobody knows, but Wes never approached Rowan again. He avoids witches in general." Her throat bobs. "Avoided."

"Surely every kid he bullied is a possible suspect, not only me," I retort.

"Yes. All students need to account for their whereabouts

last night and most of his bullied victims stayed at the academy. They avoid any place Wes goes. Unless a student hid in the woods and ambushed him…" She trails off. "Did the headteachers tell you *how* he died?"

Somebody knocks lightly on the door, and I hastily tuck my notepad into a drawer. The door opens and a woman with sleek black hair walks in, slender fingers linked together in front of her. Casually dressed in a pink blouse and gray skirt, she's older than the students, but not by much. She smiles at Holly, who doesn't speak.

"You must be Violet," the woman says in a light voice. "I'm Vanessa."

"And the academy invited you to speak to traumatized students."

Her mouth parts slightly. "Did you tell Violet I spoke to the Darwin House students in the Great Hall earlier, Holly?"

"No. I've met your sort before," I put in. "Well, someone *like* you. I once spent time with a mediator to solve issues between me and the boy I attacked at my old school." I tip my head. "How coincidental you're here when I'm accused of attacking someone again."

"Goodness, no. I'm merely here as a person any student can approach if they feel the need to talk. Tragedy affects everybody differently." Again, a serene smile. "I understand how unpleasant you must feel to be accused, and I popped in to offer you the same help."

"No need to 'pop', Vanessa. I don't need help, or for a 'supportive chat' as a guise to elicit a confession from me."

Our gazes lock. Great—Vanessa's mind is surrounded by a barrier. Not the hard wall against intrusion that I usually encounter, something squishy that absorbs my magic. If only I could read what she's thinking.

"Well, the offer stands." She nods at Holly. "And to you. Have you decided what to do about Violet yet?"

"What does that mean?" I ask sharply.

"Holly has the option whether to allow you to stay as her roommate or request you leave. Obviously, Holly might have concerns about her safety."

"She feels unsafe with me?" I ask evenly and glance at Holly, who suddenly finds the woven rug of great interest.

"I don't feel unsafe. I'm happy for Violet to stay." Holly slides me a look. "If Violet is."

"Where else would I go?" I ask. "Do I have options?"

"We're currently looking into alternatives," says Vanessa, "all that matters is everybody feels safe and happy."

I scoff. "With somebody randomly murdering students? How's that possible?"

"*One* student, Violet. Now, are you sure neither of you want to talk to me?"

"I don't 'talk' to normal people. I'm not likely to talk to *you*." I turn back to my notepad. "I have some studying to do. Goodbye."

Should I've told Holly about my theories? Because *she* might be a spy. After all, Holly attended the academy with Wesley for a number of years and barely knows the girl who's constantly rude and ungrateful towards her.

Does she trust me anymore than others?

Chapter Twenty-Two

I NEED to return to the crime scene, and I'm prepared to risk the consequences of leaving the grounds. I'm not sauntering down in the evening; befittingly I'll go in the middle of the night. There're two outcomes in this situation—I'll be noticed, or nobody will look out for me leaving because nobody believes I'd be stupid enough to return.

As I switch between sneaking and running at my vampire-half's speed from the academy to the town, I curse my parents' clever decision to ward against blood runes. At least Mr. Willis let slip the location—by a fire.

The area still smells of burned wood and the ashy remains of the blaze are disturbed by someone investigating the pile. Authorities also cordoned off the vicinity around the fire with bright yellow tape, and flowers lie close to a tree at the edge of the area. I pause and stare down at them. Wes wasn't well-liked by many, but apparently enough people cared to create a memorial.

Crouching down, I take and read each card attached to bunches of roses and sunflowers. Most contain the usual platitudes and are signed by inconsequential people, but I pull out my pen and paper to note all their names, anyway.

Amongst the flowers, there's a black cap with a red bear paw printed on the front. I've never seen anybody wearing one, including at the gathering, and Wesley definitely wasn't wearing one last night.

Significant? Again, I make a note.

Nearby voices alert me, and I drop the cap back beside the flowers as I stand and edge around the tree, preparing to run. I should've expected people would be around to guard the site.

Apart from these aren't police. Rowan and Leif, both dressed in the dark hoodies they wore last night.

Interesting.

As they duck beneath the tape, I clear my throat and step out. Leif stops dead for a moment and darts a look to the woods as if about to run, but Rowan grabs his sleeve.

"Hello, sweet Violet," says Rowan quietly as he pushes down his hood. "Are you looking to destroy evidence?"

"Why? Is that your reason for a midnight hike?" I reply and crouch to pass beneath the crime scene tape. "I doubt you're here to pay your respects."

"And you are? You forgot your flowers. There'll be bouquets in the graveyard if you want to take those?" he continues. "I hear you like visiting the place."

"I don't steal," I retort.

"Just kill?" blurts Leif, still hooded.

I make a derisive sound and walk around the ash. I'm playing my cards close to my chest—I'm not letting the pair know that I saw them last night.

But I will tell them *something*.

I cock my head at Leif. "*The situation needs dealing with.*" Then I look at Rowan. "*There'll be consequences. Are you prepared for that?*" Why is Rowan smirking? "Care to divulge what situation? Because the words 'fugitive for life' were also spoken."

Leif's eyes grow wide, and he glances at Rowan. "What are you suggesting? That *we* killed him?"

"You *were* low down on my list of suspects, but you just jumped to the top." I kick at the remains of the fire with the toe of my boot. "I would've thought the pair of you could easily throw Wesley onto the fire. Or were you disturbed?"

"Fancy yourself as Sherlock Holmes, do you, Violet?" asks Rowan and laughs.

"Offering to be my Moriarty, Rowan?" I tap my lips. "Hmm. No. I don't see you as a criminal mastermind."

"Whereas you eavesdropping in the library makes you an excellent detective?" He flicks his tongue against his top teeth. "Did you enjoy your trip to the graveyard? As if we'd meet there…"

Leif laughs too. "That's right. Rowan saw you in the library."

He tricked me? I suck my lips together. "But I know what I heard, whether you sent me on a wild goose chase or not."

"I don't think you do," says Rowan.

"Explain, then."

"Why are you here?" interrupts Leif.

"Looking for clues. Perhaps a piece of evidence to help." I tip my head towards the makeshift memorial. "What's the hat mean?"

"Hat?" Leif purses his lips and jumps the tape to pick up the item. "Huh." He holds the cap up to Rowan. "The Ursas."

"Bears?" I ask and take the hat. "Shifters?"

"You need to research more, Nancy Drew." Rowan approaches. "Do you know anything about the town?" I narrow my eyes. "No? Look into the local shifter population. There're a few clans. Ursas are one of them."

"Viggo who attacked you, Leif? Was he Ursa?" A muscle tics in his jaw—a tell I *do* recognize. "Hmm." I extract my pen and paper and make a note.

Rowan laughs at me. "You really *do* think you're a detective."

"What can I say? I like a good murder mystery. Especially when I need to clear my name." I meet his gaze. "Tell me why *you're* here, Rowan."

Ignoring me, he takes the hat from Leif, then stares at it, gripping tight. Huh?

"Anything?" asks Leif.

"Might be useful." Rowan bunches up the cap and shoves it into his hoodie pocket.

"You're stealing from Wes's memorial? You really do have a problem," I tell him.

"Tell me *you* wouldn't take the cap." He arches a brow, and I don't reply. "I thought so. This'll be more use to me than to you."

"Why?" I ask.

I hate that this guy is taller than I am because I don't like being looked down on, which is exactly what he's doing, keen eyes on mine, a smirk on his face. "We're going to check the rest of the area. I'll let you know if we find anything else."

Leif's head jerks up and his eyes take on a preternatural shine. "Move." I frown at him. "Move!"

Then I hear the nearby male voices too and don't need any more encouragement as I dart into the trees. I can still listen here.

"I wouldn't wait there," whispers Rowan as he joins me. "Shifters' senses are even better than yours. The guys will sniff you out." I narrow my eyes. "Okay. You don't have to believe me. I'm helping you."

"He's right," says Leif.

"But I want to see who this is," I protest. "And I'm not scared of a few shifters."

"Sweet, sweet Violet—"

"I suggest you stop calling me that," I bite back.

"—use your head. Attacking shifters here would not help you, would it?" With a sigh, he turns to Leif. "Let's leave Nancy Drew to her case."

The two blend into the night and I'm mad as I watch them go. Not only have they interfered, but I don't like that Rowan could be right. I can't hang around here and come nose to nose with shifters.

Muttering to myself, I edge around the perimeter, out of sight, catching a glimpse of three huge male figures. As I head away, one of them calls out to another.

"Viggo!"

Well, Rowan isn't the only one who discovered something tonight.

I don't know what games Rowan thinks he's playing with me, but I'm not joining in.

And who is Nancy Drew? A girl from the academy or town? I pull out the pen and pad and note her name.

Chapter Twenty-Three

I CONTINUE my normal activities over the next few days, so as not to arouse suspicion. Although as this involves not socializing, I wouldn't know what level the suspicion is at. Naturally, both human and supernatural investigators interview me, along with all students who attended the bonfire gathering. There appeared to be conflict between the two men over who led the interview and I left, having revealed nothing new.

A second trip into town, with the hope of sneaking away to check out the crime scene a second time, failed. Once Holly trapped me in the mall, I became so disorientated that I needed to return to the academy to get my head straight again.

I've never visited a mall in my life and that's an experience I don't want to repeat in a hurry. Each level filled with stores was a new circle of Hell, and by the time we reached the fourth floor, I threatened to set fire to the fake floral display running along the center. That way, the place could have a true Hellish feel. Holly's doubts about my mental stability are helpful sometimes—we left.

But not before I purchased my phone, which I've used for nothing apart from taking photos of the inside of books. A frustrated Holly added icons to the phone that I could click and enter the wonderland that is social media. I immediately deleted them, although I placated Holly by giving her my number, along with strict instructions not to send messages or call me. She muttered something about 'the point in you having one' and wandered off.

Frustratingly, I've had no useful encounters with any of my three suspects. Grayson avoids me and ensures I can't catch him before or after any of the classes we share. Leif barely speaks, and Rowan hasn't approached me. If I see one more smug look from Rowan... *This* is why I avoid people. They're annoying as hell.

Holly and many of the students have worn black every day since Wesley's death, which involved borrowing some of my clothes since the color isn't in her wardrobe.

"After the memorial tomorrow, you can have this back," she comments as I stare at the knitted black jumper engulfing her small figure.

"I don't mind. You look cute in those colors."

"I look like a black cloud ate me."

We smile at each other's teasing memory of the night we snuck out, then I pick up my phone. I have an issue. "Who did you give my number to?"

"Nobody," she answers. "Why?"

A sweep of her mind confirms she isn't lying.

"The messages must be a mistake then," I say, not believing that for a moment. "Have you spent time around witches recently?"

"Only in class and at the dance committee meetings." I tense, waiting for the nagging that comes every time she talks about the dance. "I don't know many other witches."

I already have my suspicions—a witch could get into her mind and a particularly *skilled* one could influence her, too.

Rowan.

I skim the messages again.

> I have something you need to see

I've ignored this for two days, despite the follow up texts.

> Meet me somewhere and I'll show you something important

> Don't you want to know what it is, Nancy Drew?

And finally, today

> Last chance. Meet me or I'll hand my special gift to someone else

I'm not accustomed to, or happy about, somebody believing they have the upper hand over me, and the messages imply Rowan does—if this *is* him.

In order to change that situation, I've a meeting to attend. One that won't end well for Rowan if he continues this attitude because I'll slice off the 'upper hand' he thinks he has.

> 8pm library

> 9pm behind the greenhouse

I grit my teeth. After this, he will *not* be in control any longer.

I leave Holly engrossed in a show, although she's watching her phone screen and sending texts more than viewing the laptop. I've prowled around the academy grounds the last few nights, and she never questions me when I leave. I've also stopped talking about my suspicions—just in case she *is* communicating with Vanessa.

The greenhouse is located towards the edge of the academy grounds in one of the darkest places on campus. As large as two classrooms, the glass building is crammed with plants, including benches with seedlings. As with Potions and Chemistry, classes taught here are Biology to humans and Horticulture to us. More specifically, cultivating rare plants needed for spells and potions.

As I joined mid-term, I haven't nurtured any seedlings and have nothing to tend to. Holly's unsuccessful nurturing led to her tears dripping onto the withered tomato plants. So, I demonstrated that my life-giving skills extend to flora. Resurrecting plants? Useless, but at least this seemed to cheer up a rainy-faced Holly.

As I stealth to the edge of the area, I tune my senses into my surroundings to avoid any chance of a 'surprise'. I pick up Rowan's scent, a mixture of sweeter smelling herbs and soap, and make to sneak up on him. Instead, a witch light flares, illuminating my way to a narrow space between the greenhouse and one of the sheds.

As I approach and Rowan comes into view, the witch flicks the light from his hand until the ball glows above him to his left.

What the *hell* is he wearing?

"Nice coat," I say. Nice *cerise pink padded* coat, buttoned up with the fur from the lowered hood touching his neck.

He smirks his annoying smirk and straightens the quilted item's sleeves. "Thanks."

"Do you have kleptomaniac tendencies?" I remain at a distance, arms crossed. "First attempting to steal my magic supplies, then a hat, and now Holly's coat."

"Which you borrowed."

"With her permission."

Rowan saunters towards me. "You certainly stood out from the crowd that night. A few people commented on your clothing choice."

"Was this exercise another attempt to rile me, or do you actually have something to show me?" I retort.

"Do you know why students normally meet here?" he asks quietly.

"I've never considered what students do in their spare time." I glance around. "A place of secrets, I imagine. A coven meeting place?"

Rowan chuckles. "Right."

"I'm not interested in joining any covens."

"Nobody's inviting you to one. Why would they?" he bats back.

"And is that supposed to upset me?" He shrugs. "Rowan. Explain why you've badgered me into meeting you. What do you have to show me?"

"Me."

I pull a disparaging face. "Really? This is a romantic overture? You're more ridiculous than I thought." Pissed that he *is* making me pissed, I turn away. "Touch me and you'll regret it."

"Hell, no. I'm not getting between you and Grayson."

"What?" I ask sharply, facing him again.

"I bet he was involved. A few of us know about his evening activities on campus. Whose idea was killing Wesley?"

The ball of magic doesn't give off much light but enough to see he's stony-faced beneath his scruffy hair.

"You're accusing me? Why? Deflecting attention from you and Leif? I know you painted runes on Wesley's floor the night you broke into my room. What's your game, Rowan?"

"Excuse me?" he retorts. "I'm not under suspicion, and I didn't paint any runes."

"Okay. But I don't *only* suspect you because I heard you and Leif planning something. I saw you hiding in the woods the night Wesley died. Then I saw you steal that cap. There's a reason."

With a sigh, Rowan unfastens the coat. "The thing is, sweet Violet." He pulls his arms out of the coat and holds the item up. "The night we met at the crime scene, I found an unusual pink coat that Dorian Blackwood's daughter wore that night. And guess what?"

The following silence irritates me as much as he does. "Is this a pause for dramatic effect, Rowan?"

"Wesley's blood is on the coat, Violet."

Rowan regards me, searching my face for any sign of a reaction. "Oh? Were you wearing the coat when you killed him?" I ask evenly.

His arm lowers slightly. "His blood. Your coat."

"Technically, Holly's. She'll be grateful you found it."

His brow dips at my continuing nonchalance. "Aren't you worried? I have a piece of evidence against you."

"Which you've kept in order to blackmail me with, since your attempt at thieving from my room failed." I smile. "And you wore the coat, thus putting your own DNA on the item. Rather stupid."

"I'm a witch, Violet. Nobody will find DNA. Magic—getting witches out of criminal convictions for many years," he replies with misguided triumph in his tone.

"Fine. Hand the coat to the investigators. If that's all you have to show me, I'll be leaving now."

My boots sound on the pavers as I turn and walk away.

"Is that it?" he calls after me. "No attempt to take the coat from me with magic?"

Again, I pause and pivot to look at him. "Is that

something you enjoy? Pain? Or are you provoking me to attack you in order to focus more attention on my violent nature?" When he doesn't reply, I stride back to him, and he looks down at me impassively. "You won't give that coat to anybody because if you *genuinely* believe I'm guilty, you know that I'll kill you before you can hand over evidence."

"I already took that risk tonight." We remain at a standstill, both looking, neither speaking. Eventually, Rowan's lips thin. "Don't you want to know where I found the coat? Why I took the cap?"

I sigh. "Okay. Where did you find the coat and why take the hat?"

"Psychometry. It's my thing."

"Your 'thing'?"

"Like necromancy is your 'thing'. Natural talent from my bloodline but weakened. I can tell you who took your coat."

Few witches practice psychometry, since not many believe it exists. But then, most never believed necromancy did either. Like future-sight, psychometry is rare and takes a lot of practice. Is Rowan telling the truth?

"You told me you're an elemental witch."

"Yes. And like you, I am elemental too. I'm not sticking to learning one type of magic."

I sigh. "Who took my coat? The murderer?"

He scratches a cheek. "Possibly. Tell me, did your meeting with Grayson in the graveyard include a romantic moment?"

"Don't be ridiculous," I retort.

"Again, the lady protests." He pauses. "If there wasn't at least a hug between you, then how's his energy imprinted on the coat?"

"Grayson's?"

"You don't look as shocked as I expected. Do you suspect him?"

"I'm unsure Grayson could replicate the rune drawn on

Wesley," I reply. "That's a *rarer* one, Rowan. One found in... let's say... old books."

"I didn't kill Wesley."

"You think Grayson did?" I frown. I'd hoped I was wrong, but I saw blood on his face. If Rowan isn't lying, Grayson could be the killer.

"Honestly, I don't know."

"Me?"

His shoulders drop. "Okay. I don't believe it was you. That's one reason I kept the coat away from authorities."

"And the other reason?"

He purses his lips at my expectant look. "I want you to help me with a spell and need to *persuade* you."

"What spell and why would I?"

"A spell that'll help Leif. You saw how people treat him. The guy deserves better. He helped me a lot against bullies—I owe him."

"I heard. But you don't strike me as a person who'd help. Not unless this benefits you, too."

"Also, power to protect myself. To become untouchable." He straightens. "Against anybody."

My mind jumps back to the book. His desperation to keep this out of my hands. The notes. Code. "What have you found, Rowan?"

"Something only a witch with Blackwood magic running through her veins can help with."

I scoff. "*That's* the reason for your clumsy blackmail attempt?"

"There's no other way to get close to you." He tosses the coat at my feet. "But take this as a gesture that I'm more interested in helping you than handing over the wrong killer. I'll help you find who killed Wesley and, in return, you can help me. Let's start with looking into Grayson."

Now this is an interesting proposition. If Rowan or Leif

are involved somehow and Grayson didn't kill, I've a perfect chance to watch and wait for them to slip up.

There's evidence out there and a reason why Rowan mysteriously possesses this coat. How could he 'find' this in the woods when authorities would've searched the whole area?

Bending and bunching the coat in my hands, I then straighten and look at him. "You had the coat with Wesley's blood on, Rowan. Perhaps the real reason you won't hand this over is that *you* killed him. There's more than a streak or two from a bloody nose on the coat."

He smiles and moves back into my personal space, so I snarl at him. "Surely, you *don't* think I'd tell you everything I know without expecting something in return?"

I lower my voice. "Walking away intact is reward enough, Rowan."

He clicks his fingers to snuff out his witch light. "You're on the right track if you suspect Grayson. If you believe I'm involved, you've derailed your investigation. Good night, sweet Violet."

My head whirls with questions as he's the one that walks away this time. "Wait!"

Rowan turns back, and his slight smile almost makes me tell him to forget it. This guy gets way too far under my skin, which has *never* happened before. "What if we got hold of something from the crime scene? Wesley's belongings would have more to detect than a coat owned by someone else—the violence would attract stronger energy."

"I did. The cap showed nothing," he replies. "Only that it belonged to Viggo."

"No. Objects taken from the scene by police. They'll be stored somewhere as part of the investigation."

"Yeah, at the police station. Are you planning to walk in and ask for them?"

"No. Take them." I haven't entirely thought through the details, but this is the answer. "Most of the town is attending this memorial tomorrow—a big show of unity between humans and supes. The station won't have many staff. I can 'persuade' someone to show me what they found."

"You're insane. What if you get caught taking evidence? That'll make you look guilty."

"I won't get caught," I say firmly. "And if I do, mental magic is my friend."

Slowly, Rowan walks over to me. "I'm coming with you."

"Why?" I ask suspiciously. "What's in it for you?"

"Plenty." He chews the side of his mouth. "Besides, two witches with superior mental magic are better than one. I've had some practice on influencing thoughts and behavior recently."

"You *did* take my number from Holly's phone! That's invasive." I sense my cheeks growing pink.

He smiles and leans down. "I love that I dig beneath your skin, Violet. All these new emotions you're showing..."

"If you're using that to weaken me, give up now."

"Feeling doesn't make you weak," he replies. "Sometimes emotions are the focus you need."

I purse my lips. "I *need* to find who killed Wesley. That's all. Then hopefully my parents will take me out of this Hell. That's pure logic, and *that's* what helps."

He shrugs. "If I've pushed past your barrier, others will, too. Then someone will take it down completely."

"I challenge *anybody* to make their way through my mental shield."

With a laugh, Rowan turns away. "That's not the barrier I'm talking about. Good night, sweet Violet."

Chapter Twenty-Four

THERE's a reason Wesley's memorial takes place in town and not at the academy. Every student is required to attend, and many of the town's dignitaries and local kids who knew him are also present. This show of unity between the town and academy is exactly that—a show. Everywhere I move, the negative energy surrounds us all.

I'm still the prime suspect but human and supernatural authorities alike are unable to touch me without evidence due to Dorian's position in the hierarchy. Neither want to upset him by falsely arresting his daughter.

Hence, I'm amongst the attendees in the town square, where students squash together on temporary long benches. They face a dais with the town's and the academy's emblems hung on either side of a school portrait of the deceased. I wonder if those who designed the town crest chose a cross on purpose before they knew crosses aren't vampire repellents? The academy's tree motif doesn't exactly scream supernatural either.

Good grief. Talk about overkill. Hardly anybody liked the guy.

I briefly chat to Rowan, but I don't tell him that I intend to visit the police station alone the moment the memorial service begins—he might take evidence to taunt me with again. Do I believe Rowan's skilled in psychometry? And would anything he discovers with magic stand up as evidence? For our authorities, yes. Humans? Less likely, thanks to phony human psychics who separated fools from their money before the real witch psychics appeared.

Grayson positions himself in the center of a bench where I wouldn't be able to reach him to talk, and I'm impressed at how well he's evaded me since the day I accused him. Several times, the guy told me he wanted Wesley dead—why doesn't anybody suspect him?

And more curiously, why didn't I pass my suspicions onto authorities when questioned? A kernel of doubt prevented me opening my mouth. What if the investigators decide 'act now, ask questions later' in order to wrap up the case? That'd take away the pressure they're under to discover the killer quickly and end badly for Grayson.

Holly watches me as I leave Rowan and I take my place beside her at the edge of the backless bench, close to the rear of the memorial service. I glance over my shoulder to where Rowan approaches Leif.

"Aha." Holly smirks at me as I meet her eyes. "Rowan!"

"What about him?"

She quirks a brow. "He's the one sending you messages. Emma *did* see you with him behind the greenhouse."

I'm rarely lost for words, but they momentarily escape me. "We were alone. How did Emma see?"

Holly gasps and shuffles closer. "She saw you both leaving. You were *alone* doing *what*?"

"Really, Holly?" I sigh.

"You do know there's only one reason people meet in that spot?" she asks.

"For privacy. Coven meetings."

She splutters a laugh. "Privacy? Yes. But more 'one-on-one' meetings. You seemed friendly with Grayson, and now you don't speak. Is that why? Rowan?"

I gawk, shifting my legs as two students squeeze past to sit on the bench, glaring at me when I refuse to shuffle along. I'm not moving from the edge of the bench; it'll be hard to sneak away if I have to push my way through people.

I'm a little exhausted by Holly's presumptions around guys, but in this case a denial might cause problems. If Violet Blackwood meets Rowan Willowbrook in secret locations for non-romantic reasons, then *why* are they meeting?

"Sorry if I'm wrong," she adds before I can reply. "I'm just excited to see you coming out of yourself, that's all. If the guys are friends, that's great you're starting to make some." She adds an apologetic smile, then makes a zipping motion over her lips.

"They're not my friends either. We have mutual interests."

Holly tips her head and her gloss-covered lips purse. "Have you not considered that those who still speak to a murder suspect are your friends?"

Why is she staring at me like that? "The guys are useful, that's all."

"And that's the only reason you interact with the people who still support you?" Her voice rises in pitch. "Because they're *useful* to you?"

A girl in front glances over her shoulder and then whispers to the one beside her. What's happening here? "Does that bother you?" She scoffs at my question. "Do you like Rowan and Grayson and think I'm treating them badly? I'm useful to *them* too. It's a trade."

"People can be a friend without expecting anything in return." She crosses her arms and looks ahead, mouth tight.

"Friendship is a confusing concept to me, Holly," I say

quietly, annoyed at the giggling from the girls in front. "According to Grayson, I'm unpleasant because I don't read body language. People confuse and frustrate me, as I do them. I prefer to depend on myself."

Holly's eyes meet mine, her cheeks flushed red. "Well, take a good look at yourself and those around because you'll notice you're depending on *more* than yourself right now."

I'm more relieved than I could ever imagine when the mayor's voice screeches through the speakers positioned beside the dais.

I'D TOYED WITH THE IDEA OF CLIMBING THROUGH A WINDOW but concluded that method of entry would be suspicious. If I come face to face with somebody and they act before I can work a spell on them, things would be awkward.

I'm correct that the station only has a skeleton staff while the memorial is in progress. There's a middle-aged woman at the front counter eating fruit from a plastic pot and she wipes her mouth before setting the spoon down. One glance at my uniform and her brow pinches, round-cheeked face souring.

"You should be at the memorial," she informs me.

Do I blend in wearing the Thornwood uniform? I'm not the only so-called goth looking girl, just the one that the academy knows is different. I tentatively scan her mind for my name, but it's not there.

"Do you only work at this desk?" I ask.

"What I do is none of your business."

But the question pulls up the thoughts I need into her mind—offices she enters to take cups of tea to the misogynistic men who believe that's her role, tidying files, fetching and carrying bags of items from and to a room.

But she never enters the morgue.

Ooh. I didn't know there's a morgue here; I presumed the authorities took Wesley to the local hospital. This is a memorial, not a funeral—maybe Wes is still in there?

This could be an even better opportunity than I realized. What if I took part of *Wesley* to Rowan instead? Psychometry extends to people. Dead people.

"Are you going to answer me?" the woman asks, interrupting my forming plans.

"I'd like to report a stolen item," I lie.

With a heavy sigh, the woman drags a clipboard from a drawer, attaches a sheet of paper and slaps it on the counter. "Fill this in." She jabs a pen at me.

I sit on a plastic bucket chair opposite the reception area, studying the doors to the back offices more than I do the paper. "Are many phones reported stolen?" I ask, doodling runes at each corner of the paper.

"They're common, yes." She doesn't look up.

"And do you find them? Will mine be here somewhere?" Still no response. "Is there anybody else here today?"

"None of your business." The woman taps on her computer. *Look at me.* I wish I'd worked more on the mind-control than necromancy.

So, I sit patiently and quietly for long enough that she finally addresses me. "Can you hurry up? You should be at Wesley's memorial. Why aren't you?"

I swallow hard and wipe the corner of my eye, adopting a hoarse tone. "I can't deal with the event. I'm too upset."

"Huh. Who'd think people like you would care?"

"People like me?" I ask softly, gently burrowing into her mind. Ah. She thinks I'm a vampire. "I care deeply." She sneers in disbelief but doesn't look away. "Can you take me to the lost and stolen property?" The woman's mouth opens and then confusion triggers inside her mind. "You know that would help me out. I'd leave you alone afterwards."

148

"You might take something."

I smile inwardly. I've squashed the 'no'. "My father's unwell and I'm waiting for a call. I'm desperate for my phone or I wouldn't ask." She closes her eyes and rubs her temples. "Please."

As my magic grows, so does the woman's confusion. This would be quicker with physical mid-control. Maybe I should've waited for Rowan. "I'm not sure."

Good grief. I stand. "But you want me to go away. You were looking forward to some peace while everybody else attends the memorial. I'm annoying you."

The woman regards me for a few moments. "One minute."

"Thank you."

Human brains are incredibly easy to scramble. A little pop at her memory afterwards and this will be fine.

"You're not expecting anybody else?" I ask.

"In an hour." She pats her pocket as she stands. "No funny business. I've a direct line to the police chief in case of trouble."

"Absolutely."

Part of the accords between supes and humans involves us *not* using any powers that influence them. That, and not killing humans. Those with mental magic skills are the most likely to slip up and use their spells for personal gain and this has been made a serious offence, alongside any unwanted energy 'consumption' by vampires—blood, physical, or sexual.

Vampires confused the humans the most once they revealed themselves. They'd never considered more than one kind of vampire exists and are unhappy all three types can walk in daylight and have no aversion to crosses or garlic. I do, but that's because it tastes gross.

Some witches and all vamps are skilled at touching minds,

something that caused issues between the two races and the shifters back in the day, and still does to a degree.

The nameless woman *isn't* the only one here—I dart past a room with a window that looks over a man at a desk. He's too focused on the papers and laptop in front of him and doesn't look up. The plaque on the door tells me he's a detective constable.

Best avoided.

We reach a flight of stairs and I hold the metal rail as our shoes tip tap down the smooth stone. Unlike the walls upstairs that are pinned with public service announcement posters, there's nothing on these apart from crumbling white paint. She pauses at a door on the left and produces a keycard to swipe.

"Is evidence kept in here too?" I ask hopefully and she nods.

Yes.

I follow into the room, but I'm more interested in what lies behind the door at the end of the hallway.

Death.

Or rather dead energy that seeps towards us, a nothingness swallowed by an invisible dark, sending unease through people's souls. Humans especially don't know why death can cause this and supes avoid it.

I'm a little dead inside, and the energy beckons to me to fill that soul with the darkness that others avoid. My parents exposed me to death from a young age, partly to show that it's natural, but also to control this thirst for the dark energy that I've inherited. My family can dampen my blood lust with a potion. My attraction to the dead? Deeply buried and untouchable.

This death aura creates a greater barrier around me than the one I construct. It's natural for humans to feel unease around me, and even if I were as bright and breezy as Holly, I'd never lose that edge.

However hard anybody rubs at the sharp edges and however much they try to teach me self-control, I'm the creation of two creatures with dark souls and dark magic. I never pretend to be anything different, although some believe I can be.

I fully embrace what I am, and understand the power, but I also refuse to act against others without severe provocation. Keeping me away from the world avoided such possibilities. I'm perfectly aware that's why my parents didn't involve me in anything outside of supernatural society until my late-teens.

Whether I intended to look for clues to a murder or not, the whisper of death ensures I'll never leave this building without stepping inside.

I stand in the other doorway, arms crossed, and watch as she wanders between two tall sets of metal shelves stocked with clear plastic boxes. A row of metal filing cabinets are placed against the wall with paper folders piled on top and a long desk beside them.

"You have a lot to do in here," I say.

The woman turns around. "Sometimes."

"No. Now." Her gaze snaps to mine and I cherry pick more thoughts. "You've an hour left to finish cataloguing evidence for the Wesley Willis murder."

That box. The one she immediately looks at. How can I take anything without being seen when the room is so small? As soon as she's placed the large box on the desk, the woman flips the lid to reveal plastic bags labeled and containing items. Folded up clothes. A phone. Jewelry. I'd love to make my way through the pile.

The grip on her mind slips a little, and she pauses, the way people do when they're suspicious. The woman glances back at me, and I flash a smile, tightening the hold on her thoughts.

You should check the shelves at the back. Count what's in each box.

The woman turns away at my mental suggestion, and I delve into the box she opened already, grabbing the first plastic bag I can get my hand around and shoving it into my skirt pocket. I've no idea what's inside, but the item is related to Wesley's murder, and that's all I need to know right now.

This is the point someone with more sense would carefully make their way from the station, leaving behind a woman who won't remember me walking into the station.

But this is also the point that death calls on Violet Blackwood.

Chapter Twenty-Five

I'VE VISITED many funeral homes but few morgues. Partly, because the smell is appalling—not death but the weird pickled-onion smell from formaldehyde, and the mix of other chemicals in the air.

I attempted to sneak into a few alone but got caught and reprimanded enough times I gave up trying. They needn't worry about me using the opportunity for necromancy—if not damaged, humans are missing a few parts that I'd need to be able to use necromancy successfully. Hearts, lungs, that type of thing. Oh, and brains—there's no point without that.

Witches have different rites after death and are always buried intact and within a day of death. Eloise first reanimated someone by accident at a witch's funeral, a strong emotional reaction triggering the magic. That's where her caution about me comes from.

There's nothing that could live again in morgues and funeral homes.

Oh. What if Wesley already *is* in the funeral home?

One way to find out.

I've stolen the woman's keycard, so she won't be able to

enter if my spell on her breaks. Her brain will unfog within ten to twenty minutes—it's impossible to know for sure, everybody's different. I need to be in and out as quickly as possible.

I flick on the eye-watering bright lights and the white, sanitized room greets me. This morgue only has a couple of tables and storage spaces for bodies—I imagine the town sees few deaths that need investigating.

I don't take long to locate Wesley.

Do I feel some sympathy for him? Nobody deserves to die horribly, even assholes who could better serve the world by not procreating. Although, I expect people could say the same about my father. I'm still struggling to accept that Grayson is the likely suspect—the supes at the elite academies are chosen for upholding the supernatural 'ways' and one of those is proving that we don't kill. I fully understand the temptation for those less in control of their natures and hemia vamps are in that category.

Wesley didn't think things through when deciding to bully creatures more powerful than him. *If* the killer is a supe and not human. There's no reason to dismiss all those at the bonfire as potential suspects.

I yank out the tray and meet Wesley's dead eyes and death mask. I'm momentarily intrigued by his appearance; he looks different to bodies prepared for a casket in funeral homes.

Don't waste time, Violet.

He's covered in a white sheet from neck to feet. I've no interest in anything apart from two things: the rune and what part of him to remove. All I have is the snapshot memory in Kirsten's mind when the poor girl found him; I bet she'll need many conversations with Vanessa. Pulling my phone from my pocket, I tentatively pull at the top of the sheet.

Dorian's right. This isn't a decently drawn Blackwood rune, neither is it one associated with death. I'd draw the rune to ward my room from unwanted visitors who'd get a major headache if they tried to step over it. Even if this was Rowan's clumsy attempt, he'd choose a relevant one.

I prepare to take a photo, and there're messages on my phone screen, from two people who've contacted me before.

where did you go?

Holly.
A second from a different number

tell me you haven't

You're not that stupid

why didn't you wait??

Rowan might follow.

I hastily take a photo of the rune and dash to the cupboard, where surgical tools hang on a wall inside. Keys. I pull out several drawers, rummaging amongst pens and stationary items. A small key is tucked away at the back of the second one that I look in.

Please be the right key.

I'm jittery as I fumble to open the cupboard, breathing out in relief as the key fits. Silver implements. Large. Sharp. That one. I grab a small hacksaw and hurry back to Wesley. Without hesitation, I saw through his little toe and place it in the small bag I grabbed from the evidence room. The toe joins a gold chain with a crucifix pendant—I've definitely no aversion to that.

Hacksaw and Wesley replaced; I move to the door, ready to slip out and check on the woman counting pointless items in the storeroom. But as I step from the morgue, I almost collide with someone. Panic spikes. Crap.

Rowan. My shoulders relax. Slightly.

"What the hell are you doing in there?" he asks, craning his head to see past me. "Bloody hell, Violet."

"Natural curiosity." I smile hesitantly.

"I hope nobody else is about to walk out. Like Wesley." He's wide-eyed and half-serious.

"Uh, no."

Rowan glances into the other room where the woman stands beside a table at the rear shelves, carefully unpacking a box. "Why didn't you wait for me? We were supposed to work together."

"Umm. You looked interested in the memorial. I thought I'd just nip in and get what I need." I pat my pocket. "So, we can go."

"'Nip in'? His cheeks begin to turn pink. "And what did you do to the CCTV?"

"CCTV?" I frown. "Nothing."

He chokes. "Violet! You can mentally affect that woman, but you can't mentally scramble a security system. You've not only stolen, but you walked into the freaking morgue. Tampering with evidence—and a body, I bet!"

"I never thought," I admit. How could I when I've barely any experience of the human world?

"You intended to waltz out of here with evidence leaving behind *evidence* of your own." He jabs a finger at a small white camera mounted high at the corner of the hallway, pointing towards the room—to us. A red light blinks accusingly.

"Oh."

"Yes, 'oh'. You've made this harder. If you'd *waited*, I could've scrambled the system before you walked into the station." He shakes his head. "This was supposed to be a quick in, mind wipe, take evidence, and out."

"And now?" I ask.

"Now I'll need to screw with the entire IT system. Corrupt

files. Disable cameras." He's glancing around, between the woman, me, and the stairs behind.

"You can do that?"

"Yeah, you need to know how to deal with human 'magic' too, if you want to outwit them." He blows air into his cheeks. "But I don't know if I'll have time. I'll need to find the bloody server first."

"This is all a foreign language to me, Rowan."

"Exactly," he says tersely. "You're smart, but also clueless."

Nearby, the woman continues her counting. I've messed up. I never mess up. "Sorry," I mumble.

Rowan straightens and stares at me. "Wow." He shakes away a thought. "Right. Watch for that camera's light going out and don't go *anywhere* until I come back."

I nod. "There's another guy in the building."

"Yeah. I'll deal with him if I need to, but you keep her mind switched off." He inclines his head. "Can you do that?"

"Yes," I retort. "Easily. Look at her."

"Do you understand the trouble we could be in if I fail? All because of your superior, bloody-mindedness?" He drags a hand through his hair. "I'm wasting time. Just wait here. I'll come back and we'll leave by the rear door. Y'know, the one we should've snuck in through."

Nodding, I glance at the woman again.

"*One* of us thinks things through," he says tersely. "And one of us almost made herself a bigger suspect."

I've apologized once; that's all he's getting. So, I nod again.

"When we leave, we go in separate directions, okay?" he says.

"You didn't need to come inside and risk implicating yourself if you knew I was already in here."

Rowan digs hands into his trouser pockets. "Yes, I did,

Violet. And not only because I want your help with a spell in return."

"Oh. Okay, then." I pause. "Why aren't you moving?"

"Aren't you going to ask why I'm helping?"

The toe feels heavier in my pocket as the seconds tick by. "You're wasting time, Rowan."

With a snort, he turns away and mutters his agreement as he heads back up the steps.

Chapter Twenty-Six

WHILE ROWAN CONDUCTS HIS VANDALISM, I remain focused on the woman, topping up the magic with a gentle caress of her mind every couple of minutes, waiting. He arrives in a semi-panic, brusquely telling me that he heard others coming into the station and we need to get out. I'm bundled through a door leading onto a back street and as soon as I step out beside the dumpster, blinking into the bright day, Rowan scoots away.

I hadn't expected him to leave me that fast—Rowan hasn't even told me if he succeeded.

I'm fortunate he decided to come into the station. That's major support to me on a lot of levels: proving my innocence, stopping me from implicating myself further, and putting himself in a situation that could end with him on CCTV alongside me stealing evidence. *Did* he manage that?

"I saw you sneaking away. What the hell are you doing, Violet?"

I jerk my head around.

Holly.

"Why did you leave the memorial?"

"I was bored?" I offer. "Why did you?"

"I'm nosey." She blows air into her cheeks. "How are you coincidentally by the police station? Have you been inside? Alone?" I rub my lips together but don't reply. "Isn't this a completely idiotic thing to do in broad daylight?" she asks. "And how did you get past... Oh. Mental magic. That'll cause trouble too! Violet..."

"I don't care if it helps clear my name."

She narrows her eyes and pulls me across the street. "What exactly were you doing? Reading the investigation file?"

Hmm. I never thought to do that; I should ask for Holly's advice more often. "No. I borrowed something from the evidence box."

"Why?"

"Reasons."

Her lips purse. "Show me what you took, Violet."

Uh oh. Toe. "I can't."

"Why?"

"I don't want to implicate you." I give a sweet smile.

Holly considers my words for a moment and flicks a look to my pockets. "Hiding evidence won't do you any favors."

"I'll return it when I'm done." I'm unsure how the coroner will explain Wesley's toe separating from his foot, but they can deal with the professional misconduct charge, I'm sure.

"Done what?" Again, she studies me and again I give a smile. "Actually, I don't want to know more. Come back to the memorial. You can't miss the barbecue." I splutter a laugh and she scowls. "Why is that funny?"

"Didn't somebody try to barbecue Wesley? That's rather insensitive of the organizers."

"Trust you to look at things that way," she says with a sigh. "Come on."

"Look at things in what way?"

THORNWOOD ACADEMY 1: NEVER SAY DIE

"Macabre."

"A memorial barbecue in the park close to where Wesley died? I'm not the macabre one." I squeeze my fingers around the plastic bag in my pocket. Not much, anyway.

Rowan hasn't returned by the time I join the masses. Ordinarily, I'd protest and sneak away again, but the whole town gathered together offers an opportunity to watch people's reactions. Possibly find another clue.

Grayson's also absent. Very telling. Can't face what he did if others speak to him about Wesley?

But that seed of doubt has flourished since Rowan told me about the coat—not only about Grayson's guilt, but whether *he's* telling the truth. I've few other leads right now, and he's possibly saved me from a lot of trouble, so I have to trust him.

The rows of barbecues and trestle tables are set up in a row, piled high with food and plates. With the smell of cooked sausages and burgers from the sizzling grills, this could be celebrating one of the human traditional holidays, but without the flags and paraphernalia.

A celebration of life.

The headteachers and town officials stand awkwardly together, and the mayor, a short stocky man who led the ceremony, comments how wonderful the spring sun is shining down on such a day celebrating Wesley's life. Gloom would be more suitable for the doom. I dutifully take my plate containing a hamburger and stand with Ollie and Holly. I detect a tension between the two lovers that's different to last time, and they're not speaking much. Suits me. At least Holly hasn't quizzed me about my trip to the police station again.

The academy kids are in their cliques and there's slight

intermingling between humans and supes, but not much. Leif is with a group of human girls near one of the trestle tables, as he often is. Interestingly, a group of shifters, including Viggo, loiter at the edge of the occasion. They weren't at the service; why are they here?

I'm not the only one watching every movement around me. The detective who interviewed me at the academy stands beside another man, both in dark gray suits, both silently eating hot dogs.

"Excuse me," I say to my friends and move over to the two guys.

The detective I recognize looks down at me, hazel eyes impassive, and takes a large bite from his bun. He doesn't strike me as somebody who'd smile much, frown lines already appearing on his forehead. Must be a stressful job. He's also grayer than the guy beside him who's human too, younger, and in a smarter suit, his brown hair clipped neatly.

Where's the witch who interviewed me alongside this dour detective?

"Any new leads?" I ask the older detective breezily.

"Violet Blackwood?" asks the man with him, bushy brows drawing together.

"Violent, more like," says the detective. "Have you seen her list of misdemeanors?"

Dorian released *those*?

"You'll notice murder isn't on the list." I lick sauce from my fingers.

"Yet." His eyes could drill into my mind if he were a witch. Instead, he's left pointlessly looking for clues to my thoughts.

"As I'm not the murderer, you must have other suspects," I continue.

"I'm not discussing the case with you. Go back to your friends." He shoos me. "I'm busy."

"I noticed you watching the shifters," I continue. "Any reason?"

Again, his gaze lands on me. "I'm *watching* anybody who has assault convictions. Shifters included."

Oh? "Assaults by shifters against who?"

"They're shifters," he says with a tinge of disdain. "They don't discriminate."

Interesting. "Has Wesley any convictions?" I ask. "Sorry, *had*."

He rubs his chin as I look at him keenly. "If you use mental magic on me, I'll arrest you *right* now, Ms. Blackwood."

The bag in my pocket suddenly feels heavier. *Toe.* "I won't. Promise."

The man beside him laughs softly.

"I'm told that Wesley was friendly with the shifters. Is that not true?" I continue.

"Little girl, please go away."

My face sours. "Your refusal to deny my question instead answers it. As does your comment about shifter behavior."

"Your *father* is fully aware that shifters behave in this way."

"Fathers," I interrupt.

He peers at me with curiosity before taking another bite from his bun. "And how about you? Any special person in your life?"

"No."

"Yet your mother is a witch with several consorts." He says the word as if they're animals. "I'm told you're friendly with the vampire, Grayson Petrescu. And we saw you with a witch boy earlier. Rowan Willowbrook?" I tense. "Strange for a girl who claims she has no friends. Did you need an accomplice in the murder?"

"That sounds very much like an accusation to me." I tip my chin. "I'll leave you to your poor detective work."

Before he can reply, I set down my plate on the table behind them and stride over to the group of shifters.

Wow, they reek when they're in a pack like this. Not an entirely unpleasant smell, just *potent*. Viggo hulks over me—he's intimidating close up too, a scar above his lip and amber eyes that are decidedly unwelcoming.

"I never introduced myself the other night. I'm Violet."

He frowns for a moment and then laughs, looking to his gathered friends to join in with him. "You're not my type, sweetheart."

"Shame. Who do you think killed Wesley?"

The laughter cuts dead. "We heard a vicious little girl called Violet did."

"And do *you* think that?"

Viggo crosses his arms, the disdain smearing his face. "Supes are ready to kill each other at the drop of a hat. Could be any of you."

"Does 'supes' include shifters?" I ask.

"We're not like them." I look to a gruff guy to my right. Although as tall as Viggo, he's lither and stance less aggressive. "But we don't appreciate humans treating us as if we are."

"Ah. The old prejudices stand." I look around me, at the segregated groups. "And so, you dislike humans too?"

"What are you trying to say?" growls Viggo.

"Wesley was rather rude about supes on the night in question. I presume that annoys you if he said you're part of our society."

Viggo leans down and I can smell the meat on his breath. "I don't like what you're implying, *Violet*."

"Viggo and Wes were mates," puts in a third guy.

"Mates? How's that possible? Wes is human. And male. Procreation isn't possible."

Viggo laughs and jerks his head at me, looking at the

others. "Thinks she's funny, Rory," he says to the other guy who spoke.

The third stumbles and I'm annoyed when a human guy knocking into Rory cuts short my interrogation. "Watch it, jerk," Rory snaps.

"Why are you here?" asks the human icily.

I never had a close look at the guy last night, but I'm sure this is Kai—same build. I pull out my phone. "Kai, right?"

"Yeah," says Viggo, eyes now fixed on the intruder. "Thanks."

"Why are you putting my name into your phone?" asks Kai and looks at me as if I'm crazy.

"Aww. Perhaps the little goth girl likes you." Rory nudges him hard.

Kai sneers and knocks him in return. "You should leave. You've no right to be here."

"We like a good barbecue," says Viggo with a smirk. "Not impressed we weren't invited."

"Maybe because you kicked the mayor's son unconscious a few months back." Kai shoves at him. "He's still in the fucking hospital."

"The asshole tried to touch my girl," Viggo snaps.

I sigh quietly. How pathetic.

"You can't stop shifter girls hooking up with humans," snaps Kai. "And she wasn't *your* girl. Lacey was trying to keep away from you."

"Yeah. Well. We don't appreciate any who step out of line." He shoves Rory out of the way and looks down at Kai. "You *all* need to remember that. This land belonged to us first."

Again, I tap a note. "How long ago was that?" I ask.

Viggo's head snaps around. "What?"

"I'm making a note for my history project."

"Bullshit."

"Two hundred years ago," puts in Kai. "Your *elders* don't care."

"Some do. This is and always has been *our* land," growls Viggo. "Bad enough humans act like they own the place, but rebuilding that academy after so many shifters died in that location is an insult."

Damn, this is interesting. "So... you didn't like Wesley, Viggo?"

Viggo's eyes narrow, his cheeks now splotched with red. "Tolerated. I heard he did good work inside the academy, so we left him alone. And I don't mean studying."

"The bullying?"

"I'd call it keeping people in line."

"Were you keeping Wesley in line and things went too far?" I suggest.

"Watch your mouth," he snarls.

Ooh. Strong reaction.

"Don't threaten Blackwood's daughter," says Rory, and slaps him on the back.

"That vicious bastard has no jurisdiction over shifters. *That* was part of our race's agreement." He leans closer still. "I don't give a fuck who you are, sweetheart."

I wipe the spittle from my face. "I very much think you should, asshole."

From the corner of my eye, I see the detectives watching keenly, the younger one with hands in his pockets. They're not the only ones—the area is blanketed with silence. Mr. Willis makes a move towards us, but the detective steps in his way.

We've drawn too much attention, but I don't care. Viggo's hand jerks towards my neck and I step to one side, shooting mental magic into his pea brain.

Viggo snarls and steps back, both hands on his head. "Small dick energy?" I ask him.

"Get hold of the bitch," he says, voice too low for the rapt crowd to hear.

Viggo's not-so-little minions attempt to take hold of me, too. One's grabby hands come towards me until my magic smacks his head and he reels. I'm caught off-guard as a second steps forward, grabs and lifts me by my upper arms, until I'm looking into Rory's half-bearded, unpleasant face.

"You don't know who you're dealing with," he says, voice laced with pointless menace.

"I believe you should spend more time looking into our society and what a hybrid is," I say, as he continues to hold me off the ground. "Then you would know exactly who *you're* dealing with."

Flames flicker at my fingertips by my sides, and as I glance at them, he looks down, too. "See where my fingers are close to?" I whisper. "I'd hate if you suffered burns in that region. Serious brain damage if I singed your dick."

"What the fuck?" He drops me to my feet, the menace in his voice replaced by panic.

And then I realize how much I love this.

These powerful, arrogant guys reduced to terrified boys as they look at the flames circling my hands and growing by the second. Damn, I wish I still had my familiar; the trio would run screaming.

As the three stumble back, I make a sudden move forward, flames flaring higher, and laugh as they recoil further. "What's wrong?" I lunge a second time. "Am I getting close to the truth?"

"You're getting close to a fucking target on your back," spits Viggo, eyes on my hands the whole time.

"And you think your threats worry me?" I call out.

His face twists in fury as I laugh at him and conjure my fire into a ball. If any try to move, I've some handy mental

167

magic to hold them in place. I'll keep going until the assholes back down. If I have to singe them a little? So be it.

Somebody seizes me from behind, pinning arms to my side, and I yell out, the flames vanishing as I summon a barrier against my new assailant. "Get the f—"

"Stop doing this in front of the whole bloody town, Violet," Leif interrupts, half-whispering in my ear. "In front of detectives. Don't you have any self-control?"

"Let me go or it'll be painful for you," I grit out.

"Promise you won't touch the shifters."

Like *he's* touching me. This guy's body practically engulfs mine, and the shock weakens my spell, his muscular power absorbing the magic barrier. Nobody has weakened me this acutely for years—not since enormous Ethan carried his furious young daughter away from her latest magical misdemeanor.

"Fine," I say through gritted teeth. "Put me down. Now."

Leif releases me, but one hand remains lightly on my shoulder. None of the gang pay attention now my fire's out, their focus switched to Leif.

"Might've guessed *you'd* jump in and help a fucking witch," snaps Viggo. "Or are you using her as a shield, you traitorous bastard? How pathetic."

I land on my ass on the grass as Leif roughly shoves me to one side, making a sudden move on Viggo. Viggo parries Leif's blow and his fist collides with Leif's face. Bone cracks and blood spurts from Leif's nose, a hushed whisper rippling through the crowds.

Leaping to my feet and taking ragged, angry breaths, I focus on the fury this time, allowing it to pool in my veins. Kicking people unconscious? Controlling girls? I'm ready to hit them with enough pain that their screams will be heard at the other end of town.

The whole group suddenly stumbles as the ground

beneath their feet begins to tremble, jagged cracks appearing where they stand. Leif swears and snatches my arm, moving at shifter speed away from the localized earthquake rumbling around the shifters.

Localized earthquake. As Leif holds me to him again, I look between all the witches still present. Some are elemental focused, but who would bother helping me?

Rowan. On the edge again, as he always is.

He stares at the group, gray clouds gathering above where he stands behind the crowd, clenched fists by his side, a vague glow of magic around him. Everybody else is transfixed on the spectacle as our eyes meet.

Rowan's familiar triumphant smile slides across his face as he flicks his fingers open, still looking at me. A sudden wind pushes the clouds forward, until the gray bursts into rain over the shifters' heads.

The shifters yell, as the water drenches them, and a silent, shocked group watch. With a nod at me, Rowan slips away, leaving behind chaos and wet shifters sliding in mud, who're trying to avoid the widening crevices.

Sudden. Intense. Absolute. Rowan wasn't joking about his elemental powers.

I turn to the detectives who've appeared at my side. "Any new suspects?"

Chapter Twenty-Seven

I'M happy I've finally found the chance to speak with Leif alone but not entirely impressed by the reason why. A visit to the headteachers would be better than my current position—waiting outside Vanessa's room. The headteachers are currently questioning all elemental witches present at the memorial, excluding Rowan who'd left unnoticed. He returned to the scene a few minutes later, claiming he'd visited the bathroom.

As I'm a 'victim' of the altercation, along with Leif, I've the dubious pleasure of discussing my distressing encounter with the counselor. Somehow, I think my next encounter with Viggo and his gang will be more traumatic.

If I were able to be traumatized. I've not experienced this state, but I've heard the word many times, especially when younger: "Violet. You traumatized the poor child." My fascination with evoking strong emotions in people led to trouble; I no longer traumatize others for fun.

Leif hunches forward, arms dangling between his legs as he stares at the floor, either lost in his own mind or ignoring me. A few of the guys look odd in school uniforms, their mature bodies unnaturally constrained in the same clothing as the younger students. Leif's one of those, like he's a dressing up to blend into his environment but achieving the exact opposite.

"Why are you staring at me, Violet?" Leif turns his tired eyes to mine.

"I was thinking how out of place you look."

He makes a soft, scornful noise. "The only shifter, here? Yeah."

"No. In those clothes. You don't have a child's body, therefore you look unusual." I nod at his wide thighs.

"Is that right? And do you pay much attention to my body, Violet?" he asks with a half-smile.

"Only to deduce the weakest spots so that if you touch me again, I know where to strike."

"Oh, man." Leif shakes his head and laughs, returning to staring at his feet. "I only took hold of you to avoid trouble, Violet."

"And you've gotten yourself involved," I add. "I had things in hand, Leif. The shifters would lose against me."

"That's the problem. Or could've been." He looks back up. "Losing control wouldn't be good for you."

"I was *in* control. I'm *always* in control."

"But you can't control people around you, Violet."

This time, I laugh at him. "Yes, I can. Dead or alive."

His brow pinches. "Yeah, I know all about witches' and vamps' mind-control. Saw Rowan using that once, and I've been careful around him ever since."

"Mind controlling who?"

"Guess. Wesley almost jumped off the highest roof of the academy. Never bullied Rowan again." He chuckles. "Wes pissed himself."

"Oh." Eww. "*That's* what happened. Holly mentioned something vague."

"Not many people know because Wes threatened the few who saw. Rowan told me; I keep quiet. Man, I wish I'd been there. Bastard deserves everything he got."

"That's an odd way to speak about someone who died recently." I fight against getting my notepad from my pocket, least of all because I've stolen items, and the deceased's toe might fall out. "You hate Wesley that much?"

Leif shrugs. "Didn't deserve to die, but I'm glad he's gone."

Wow. I thought *I* was the heartless one. A shifter trait?

"Why do you care if I get into trouble and lose control?" I ask him.

He tips his head, hair sliding to one side. "I don't want you to get hurt, Violet."

"Because then I can't help with your escape plans?"

"You think that's the only reason I look out for you?" I frown. He's confusing me. A lot. "We're outsiders, which I struggle with, and that you embrace. I love that about you. Don't change and let the bastards get you down."

Love that about me? "You love that I'm an unpleasant, dark-hearted girl?"

Leif's cheeks dimple as he smiles. What is he trying to say? "You're… unique. A puzzle. I like puzzles."

"So do I. Not jigsaws. Other puzzles." Leif shakes his head at me and laughs. "What?"

"Do you think you'll ever let anybody close to you, Violet?"

"Physically? Like you held me before?" I arch a brow.

"No. Get close to *you*."

"Now you're sounding like Rowan." I purse my lips and he smirks. "*Now* what's amused you?"

"Rowan and you. Similar people. Nice little arrogance and sarcasm barriers to keep people away. Dig beneath and you'll find he's a nice guy with a little too much power. You've certainly attracted his attention, and nobody attracts Rowan's attention."

I straighten. "Are you implying I should be grateful for his attention? He takes great pleasure in annoying me."

"You know how little boys pull little girls pigtails to get their attention? He's pulling yours."

"What on earth are you talking about? You're making no sense. At all. I don't even have pigtails."

Leif sits back and places both hands on his knees. "Well, thanks for checking up on me the night the shifters attacked, anyway."

Is that what I was doing? Maybe the outsider connection is there. *Something* sent me trailing after his blood.

I pause to consider my next words. "Rowan admitted you met in the woods the night Wesley died. Why?"

"No idea why Rowan was there." I don't need any help in knowing *that's* a lie. "But he found me after I left the fire."

"Before or after somebody else attacked you?" I tip my head. "You couldn't stand up when I saw the pair of you, and the nurse was worried enough to keep you in the infirmary."

Biting his fist, Leif looks down again. "Things are a bit hazy, but I'm sure I'd remember if I'd fought with anybody else."

"There's a possibility you *might've*?" I press.

He frowns at me. "You accusing me of killing Wesley?"

"No, I—"

"You know what, Violet? I've defended you when others pointed the finger at the Blackwood kid. Now you accuse me? I'm not a pawn in your murder-mystery story; I'm a person and I don't like you accusing me of shit." I'm taken aback by his sudden forceful words in contrast to our earlier conversation. "And don't you *dare* say my reaction 'puts me at the top' of your suspect list."

Hmm. Shifter temper: I've met *that* a few times. I nod,

173

cross my arms, and turn away from him, fingers itching to make notes. Instead, I take my phone out.

A message from Rowan. Good.

Tonight?

sooner the better where?

my room

uh no

you want to risk public with the stuff you have?
Either that or I come to yours

An annoyingly accurate point.

no Holly will be there. don't you have a
roommate?

Nope

Huh. Unfair.

ok if I can get out of here

you in trouble?

I'll see you later

when

8?

"Now, who'd like to speak to me first?" Vanessa stands with her hand on the open door to her room. She's casually dressed in a long, floating skirt and shirt, both patterned with tiny flowers, and wearing a wide, open smile I'm sure they taught her at 'counselor school'.

"Violet first," says Leif brusquely. "She's eager to leave me."

As I expected. Sofas that swallow you, scattered with cushions, a box of tissues on the low table, and something cloying that's supposed to be a relaxing scent. I glance around. Ah. Scent from one of those weird human things—bottles with sticks jutting out that are inexplicably used to spread fragrance.

Behind Vanessa's comfy chair are shelved books. I don't need to read the spines to know they're all connected with human psychology in some way.

"Do sit, Violet." Vanessa gestures at a yellow sofa, so I shove aside a red cushion and perch on the edge. "How are you feeling?"

"Fine. Can I go now?"

She pulls a sympathetic face. "Despite your abilities, the threats and physical assaults must be upsetting."

"Not really. Again, can I go? I've things to do." I pause. *Actually...* "Do shifters often cause trouble that upsets humans?"

"I'm only concerned about students who attend Thornwood." She places both hands on her knees. "We've had issues, yes, which is why you must report if anybody threatens you again."

"I will." Not. "Any closer to finding the killer?"

She blinks rapidly. "I'm not involved in police matters."

"Hmm." I look to the small window and the daisies in a clear vase on the sill. "I hope they find the culprit soon so authorities can stop focusing on me. If I'd killed Wesley, everybody would know. I would've reanimated the bully and insisted he performed tricks."

I look back. Vanessa's neutral mask has slipped. "The necromancy."

"Mmm." I flash a smile.

"You talk about this a lot despite your other magical skills, yet haven't practiced that magic."

"Um. How would I? Apart from Wesley, nobody has died. Nobody in my vicinity, anyway."

"And you'd use the skill should that opportunity occur? You're capable?"

"Is this human nosiness or a request?" I rest back on the sofa.

"Curiosity. It's almost as if you enjoy the effect on people when you tell them you're a necromancer, rather than possessing the actual ability." She smiles. "A barrier."

Good grief. "Thank you for your psychological evaluation. I'll ensure you're first to meet anybody I reanimate."

A silence as deathly as that in the morgue follows, and I again try to probe her mind. She's as squishy as the sofa. "Are you a supe?" I ask her.

"Yes. Half-witch. Looks like we have something in common—both hybrids. Is that why you're friendly with Leif? The hybrid connection?" She slants her head.

"And the humans are okay with that?" I ask, ignoring her.

"My employers are, yes."

"Vague."

"You never answered my question."

"Did Leif sound friendly a few minutes ago?" I ask.

"No. Does that bother you?"

"No." I hold her gaze. What *bothers* me is the physical hold he had on me earlier.

"That's something I believe you should talk about, Violet —coping with how people perceive you."

Is she deranged? "Firstly, I don't care how I'm 'perceived', and secondly, I want to leave now."

"No man is an island, Violet."

What the hell? This interview needs ending now. "Is that a cliche or are you a fan of poets from the Romantic era,

Vanessa? Not my favorite literary period. I'm rather partial to Shakespeare—I do love a good tragedy." I stand. "I once lived on an island, Vanessa, and would be happy to do so again."

Frustration is one of the few emotions I've learned to read. I often see this on people's faces, along with a desire to move far away from me. "How educated you are, Violet," she says tersely. "And how *much* you believe in your superiority."

I give her my sweetest smile. "My father has a fondness for reading. He likes quotes too and always said 'knowledge is power'. I've inherited many of his qualities."

"Yes, Violet. That's what we believe may be the problem."

For the school or me?

Chapter Twenty-Eight

I'VE ONE GOAL TONIGHT — visit Rowan and find out what secrets these items hold. Vanessa and her pointless chat wasted enough time; the authorities want a culprit in custody quick and the scrutiny will return to me if they get nowhere with their investigations.

I return to my room and pause. Odd. Holly's plush pigs are thrown around the room. Pushing a couple out of the way with my shoe, I change from my uniform into black leggings and a knee-length dress with black lace at the hem and sleeves, then slip on a matching cardigan that falls to my knees. My make-up needs a touch up too, but as I pull out a kohl pencil, I startle when a loud sniff comes from the corner of the room.

The lump beneath the pile of blankets on Hollys's bed moves. Another intruder? When I walked in, I'd presumed this was a pile of items she'd inexplicably filled her bed with.

But the sniffing?

Holly emerges from beneath the fawn-colored chenille blanket with anguish I haven't detected since a family friend's cat died. I re-animated said cat, but June wasn't impressed despite my success. The creature had all four limbs, a head, and a tail, but she didn't like its new appearance or its new desire to hide in high places and ambush her.

Again and again, I find people ungrateful for my help. Every necromancer needs practice, so of course the results wouldn't be perfect. I understand she doesn't like the scars from the cat's daily attack, but how was I to know that Mr. Fuzzybutt would no longer have a fuzzy butt? Or any fur at all?

"What's the matter?" I ask Holly. Tears aren't difficult to interpret, and her painfully upbeat energy isn't screaming through the room.

Holly stares at me and her eyes brim before she drags in a breath and makes a noise somewhere between a wail and a howl.

Alarmed at the noise, I drop the kohl pencil and grasp at the reason. "The memorial? Has that upset you?"

Holly shakes her head.

"Um." I rub my head. "The death?" I scour my mind. "Your Biology grade? I can help with—"

"Ollie!" She stares numbly ahead and spits his name; I turn my head, expecting him standing in the doorway.

Nobody.

Oh, no. "Did he die?" I ask.

"No." She drags in another breath. "*No.*"

Ah. I should've noticed the significance of the stuffed pink creatures tossed around the room, encroaching into our no man's land. "He *upset* you."

Reddened eyes turn to mine. "I don't want to talk about it."

Now I'm completely confused.

"Would you like me to do something?" I ask.

She sniffles and hugs one of her surviving pigs closer. "Do you have any chocolate?"

"I was thinking more along the lines of a hex, but okay." I wrinkle my nose. "Sorry, I don't have chocolate."

One part of my mind can't focus on this exchange, instead fixated on my upcoming meeting with Rowan. Another part is pulled to stay and talk. A week ago, I would've excused myself and left. A week before *that*, probably just left.

But this isn't fair. Holly shouldn't cry. Not only because I've no ability to stop the tears but because someone's wiped away the Holly whose happy energy fills the academy.

How odd that the situation bothers me.

"Did he…" I pause, attempting to find words that won't make her cry harder. 'What happened?"

Her jaw clenches. "Ollie doesn't want to date anyone from the academy anymore."

"Why? Has he…" *Don't say it, Violet.*

"Cheated?" Her face crumples again. "I don't know! Ollie said that anybody involved with academy kids is being threatened."

"So, he's a coward?"

She blinks. "I can't mean anything to Ollie, or he'd ignore them."

"Hmm. Or maybe he's frightened." I purse my lips. "Did he say who was responsible for the threats?"

The wet-cheeked, red-eyed girl glares. I think. "Why? Want to add their names to your investigative journal?"

"Good point. That hadn't crossed my mind until you mentioned it." She sinks back on the bed and sobs again. "I'm curious, that's all. Especially if there're people putting a wedge between town and academy."

"Would you hurt the people responsible?" she asks warily.

"Do you want me to?" No response. "Do you want me to do something to *Ollie*?"

"Give him a backbone," she mutters.

"He already has one. Would you like me to remove it instead?"

Holly chuckles and sits. "Violet. It's okay. I know you're headed out somewhere this evening. I don't expect you to stay here and listen to me." She smiles weakly. "I'm not sure you could help, anyway."

I sit on the edge of my bed. "I could find chocolate?"

"Why are you being nice?"

Good question. Is Rowan right? Has mixing with people torn a small hole in my barrier that means I care?

No. Not others. *Holly*. "You helped me," I say. "I didn't want or need the help, but you did. So now I'll help you."

She sniffs loudly and half-laughs. "Like I said at the memorial, people are helping you now, even if you don't notice."

Helping. Friend.

Oh.

"At the memorial. Were you talking about yourself when I spoke about Leif and Rowan as useful? Is that what upset you?"

Look at me, deciphering human code.

"Sort of."

I sigh. "Sorry. I don't like somebody treating you this way, Holly. What do you want me to do to Ollie?" Her eyes widen. "Maybe not the spine thing. Nothing permanent or serious, though. I've a murder charge to deal with."

Her shoulders droop to match her mouth. "Don't hurt Ollie. It's okay. He doesn't deserve that."

"Ollie doesn't deserve your tears. The tomato seedlings did, but not a guy." I smile.

With a pout to cover her returned smile, Holly throws the pig she's holding at me. The thing lands on the floor, so I pick it up.

"A minor hex?" I suggest.

"No, Violet." I toss the pig back to her. "But it's sweet of you to offer."

I shrug. "I'm all for revenge—family trait. I hope Ollie didn't physically hurt you or cheat."

"No, otherwise I *would* be asking for your help."

"Just so you know, I do take things literally, so if you ever ask, please be specific and clear about what you want me to do to him." I pat my pocket to ensure I swapped the items from my skirt to my jeans. "I have to meet Rowan now."

"Oh?" She wipes her eyes with the back of her hand. "Where?"

"In his room. There's something we can't do in public." I pause. "Why are you looking at me like that?"

"I'm not saying anything. Just..." Holly chews her lip. "Be careful, Violet. Rowan's... odd. He has this weird vibe."

"Like the vibe I supposedly have with Grayson?" I arch a brow, slightly relieved the tears stopped. "Is *he* weird?"

"No weirder than most vamps. Unapproachable. Short-tempered. Not a fan of humans," she says. *Apart from their blood?* "Although, I like that he looks out for the other supes against bullies. He must be an okay guy."

"Hmm." I glance at the door. Or a murderer. "I'll ask Rowan if he has any chocolate and if he does, I'll bring you some."

Holly chokes a laugh. "Don't hurry back if you have things to do."

"I won't." I walk over to the door and pause before looking back. "I'm sorry if I upset you at the memorial. I do appreciate your friendliness."

"Violet. That's alright. I want to help you settle into the academy and—"

"I don't want to settle," I interrupt. "I can't leave Thornwood until the killer is caught, but as I am staying, I'm glad I share a room with you."

"Why?" Holly studies me, then sinks back on the bed again. "I can never tell what you're thinking, Violet."

I smile. "Why am I glad I share a room with you? Because you're my friend."

In the hope this stunned, silent response is a positive sign, I walk from the room.

I *think* Holly and I meet her definition of 'friends.' I've yet to figure out exactly what that is, but I like her. Maybe cruelty to animals isn't the only thing that upsets me. Perhaps there's more of my mother in me than I accept—or have allowed.

Still, the offer stands. I'll take revenge on Ollie if she wants; I have practice at that sort of thing.

Chapter Twenty-Nine

"Holy crap, Violet." Rowan's face blanches as I tip the contents of the bag onto his bedroom floor.

"I've never understood that phrase," I reply.

"Is that a toe?" he asks hoarsely, then looks up. "Wesley's toe?"

"Yep. There's a signet ring, too. And a pendant on a chain." I poke at the collection.

"What the hell were you *thinking*?"

"That a part of Wesley would work best for your psychometry?" I suggest. He's still pale, eyes wide. "Or not?"

"I'm not touching it!" He drags a hand through his hair. "Are you telling me Wesley's body is now missing a toe?"

I frown. "Evidently."

He holds his head in his hands, then looks up. "Don't you *think* someone might be suspicious if he has body parts missing? Violet!"

"Calm down. I'll put the toe back tomorrow. Not like the guy's going to *miss* it."

Rowan chokes out a laugh. "And reattach it how? There's no magic that can do that."

I shrug. "Authorities would think the toe fell off?"

"I knew you were weird, but this is insane, Violet." He pushes the toe back to me with a pen. "Please put this away. God, I can't believe I'm saying these words, but take the toe back tonight. I doubt the humans fixed the damage to their IT system and security yet."

"I'm sorry if I got this wrong, but I *need* to know who killed Wesley and then we can work on exposing him or her," I retort.

"The ring and necklace would work," says Rowan. "Why didn't you tell me you'd done this? I could've stopped your crazy act."

"Crazy act? You interrupted Wesley's memorial with a sudden seismic event and a storm."

"Because *you* were about to attack somebody in front of dozens of witnesses." He huffs. "You'll have to pray that one of the shifters doesn't die next."

My back goes ramrod straight. "What?"

"If someone is trying to frame you for one murder, they might do it again. That *someone* might plan to kill off a few people. I bet this is all about your father. Pass me the chalk." He points at his desk.

About Dorian? "I've added the shifters to my suspect list," I say as I hand him blue chalk. "Did you hear some of the things they said? What if they're trying to stir up trouble between the academy and humans?"

Rowan purses his lips as he chalks a circle. "Please put that toe away before I vomit."

Rowan's room appears exactly as I expected—like him. Chaotic and messy but in that way some people prefer to live. A space where he could still locate exactly what he wanted straightaway, as if the piled books or strewn items are actually carefully placed. Goodness knows how he manages to use his bed unless he sleeps on *top* of all the books.

His mind must be the same; Rowan's sharp and always locates the right words and actions without rummaging around too much.

"Is the book you stole from the library in that pile?" I point to the slew of reading material. "I still want to read that book. Does it contain answers to your code?"

"What code?" He frowns.

"Didn't you make notes in margins in other books?"

He visibly shudder. "I *hate* when people deface books. Monsters."

I agree with his sentiment but I'm annoyed if this is true. "Will you show me the book?"

"Yeah. Sometime. If you ask me nicely." There's that smirk, and here's my scowl. "I don't like my family's grimoires stuck on library shelves."

"Which is what you meant by 'yours' that day?"

"Precisely. You digress, Violet. Let's do this."

"One more question. Have the heads spoken to you about the incident at the memorial yet?" I ask.

"No. I left the scene, remember? How much trouble were *you* in?"

"Sent to Vanessa. Anyway, my response was self-defense."

"Of an extreme nature." He smiles at me. "You need to be more subtle."

I drop the chain into the middle of the circle and place the ring in the center. "How?"

"True." He chuckles. "I doubt you're capable of subtlety."

"I had the situation under control, Rowan. I didn't need help."

"Yes, you did. Like you needed help at the station, and like you need help now." He gestures at his spell circle. "Did you give Holly her coat?"

"Couldn't get the blood off. Burned it." He rubs his temples in despair. "*Subtly.*"

I study Rowan more closely and consider Leif's earlier words. Seems all the outsiders are attracted to me, and I mean in a magnetic sense, not physical. I think. His thick aura feels lighter tonight, more relaxed in his own space. Leif talks about sarcasm and arrogance and Rowan's definitely skilled at both; I never considered looking beneath that.

Rowan's help at the police station. Sure, he wants me to assist him with his own spell in exchange for this one, but Rowan took a risk—what if he failed in messing up the CCTV and was implicated?

He glances up, aware of my scrutiny and I look back into his steel eyes—steel to protect himself as well as in color. But he's softer. Less of that smirk that often hovers around his lips.

"Why are you staring at me?" he asks.

"That's what Leif asked me earlier, too. I'm just considering you may not be as big an asshole as you seem."

Rowan snorts a laugh. "I must be slipping."

"If I had pigtails, would you pull them?" I continue.

"Huh?" He rubs his cheek, and for once his expression is readable. Surprise. "Is this a weird kink?"

"Excuse me?" I retort. "Leif told me you wanted to because that's what boys do to girls they like sometimes. Or something. He confused me."

Rowan continues to stare at me as if I've grown another head. "I doubt you'd entertain me touching your hair, let alone pulling."

"Correct."

"Doesn't stop me thinking you're awesome, Violet." He smiles. An actual smile, not a smirk. "You're a force of nature and it's fucking amazing."

"I find *your* nature based magic greater."

"Is that a compliment?"

"Is calling me awesome?"

He holds my look. "Yeah."

"You are a confusing boy. Can we just do the spell?" I shuffle around, irritated by his small talk.

He shakes his head. "I'm not a boy, Violet."

"Fine. Guy. Or whatever you want to be. Spell?"

With a sigh, Rowan picks up the chain and examines it, dangling the pendant in front of his face. "I need to perform a spell on the items and then I'll need your help."

"Right. And if you don't get any answers from them, will you consider the toe?" His disparaging look answers for him. "No. Okay."

Placing a hand on either side of the items inside the circle, Rowan speaks an incantation I've never heard, and I can barely hear him. "Secret?" I ask.

"Shush."

He *shushed* me?

The magic energy around Rowan isn't as recognizable as earlier, but there's a stronger presence in the room than the last witches I attempted to work with. "Aren't you tired after your grand spell earlier?" I ask as he removes his hand.

"A bit, but it takes a lot to exhaust my magic. That's how I can practice more." He rubs his hands together. "More energy than you have as a hybrid, it seems."

"Are you saying I'm weaker than you?"

"Hell, no. Not once you add in your vamp side." He picks up and dangles the chain again. "Do you think that's why you're... how you are? Like, your brain isn't normal too?"

"Is anybody 'normal'?" I retort. "Isn't one person's perception of normal based on their own beliefs? To me, *you're* not normal. To others, I'm a psychopath—which I take offence at, by the way. My father is a borderline psychopath, *I'm* a sociopath. There's a difference."

He smiles. "You just proved my point, Violet."

"At least I know and accept what I am."

"Fair enough. But I don't think your father is a

psychopath, otherwise he wouldn't love and care for others in his life. People throw the word around too much. Deranged and dangerous at times? Yes. Psycho? No."

"You've evidently never met him."

Rowan sighs. People at this academy do seem to sigh a lot around me. Then he squeezes the ring and chain in one hand and holds his other towards me. I stare. "Hold my hand."

Rowan may as well have told me to undress in front of him. "I can't do that!"

"I washed them." He fights a smile. "I need your Blackwood magic to boost mine."

"You said you had enough energy." I sit on my hands.

"But yours will sharpen mine. Don't you *want* to see what the objects hold, Violet?" I run my tongue along my top teeth. "I won't touch you anywhere else."

"I wasn't suggesting you would."

"Although the invitation to your bed the other night held promise," he teases.

"I'm not interested, Rowan."

"In me, or in anybody at all?"

"Anybody."

"Cool. Then I won't take it personally." Rowan beckons with his spare hand. "Violet."

No. Our magic will connect, synchronize, and we'll be wrapped together as one for the whole time we touch. That's *as* intense and invasive as a more intimate entanglement.

But he knows I've no choice; without this I've less chance of moving my investigations forward.

"How long do I need to hold your hand for?" I ask.

"Can't predict. But stop whenever you want." He's sincere, despite all his weirdness.

"Can't be long. If you insist I return the toe tonight, I'll need to leave."

"The toe..." he mutters. "Cast aside for a toe."

"What?"

"Just hold my hand, Violet."

I've held my mother's hand while practicing magic—even though my parents aren't allowed to touch me either and respect my wishes—so I know exactly what to expect.

Only I don't expect what actually happens once our fingers link.

The jolt of energy from Rowan flows as quickly to me as mine to him, charging through my veins, combining and growing. I catch my breath, eyes widening as his meet mine with equal shock. His fist holding Wesley's items glows with a blue light, as do our linked hands, and the surging magic floods my senses until I'm no longer aware of where I am.

Everything Rowan sees projects into my mind as our hands lock together, chained by the magic.

Wesley wore this ring for years. Rowan sweeps away images from the distant past, pushing through time until he hits the night Wesley died. He laughs softly as he sees my exchange with Wesley beside the fire as the images flick onwards.

The object can't pick up scents or sounds, only energy and images. We move past the moments with Leif and Viggo and into the woods, where the next surroundings bring something new, growing thicker and darker. A light bobs ahead of Wesley, growing closer, but the attack comes from behind.

Wesley lands on his front but someone turns him onto his back, and pain screams through him as the attacker descends. Only his attacker's eyes are visible, a scarf wrapped around his face, and I mutter frustration under my breath.

The scene fades and someone different leans down, looking into Wesley's fading eyes.

Grayson.

Then nobody. Nothing but the sense somebody stands

close by. I'm rigid, as if experiencing Wesley's emotions as the darkness of death envelops him.

Something else. Terror infuses the ring, but a different energy hovers around.

Triumph.

Chapter Thirty

I TEAR my hand away from Rowan and cradle it to my chest as if he burned me. "No," I say hoarsely. Rowan doesn't respond, merely stares at me. "I can't believe Grayson would kill. And why would he frame me?"

Still, Rowan stares blankly at me, his cheeks red, and he drops the objects from his hand onto the floorboards. "Fuck," he says eventually.

"I have to find Grayson. Now. He needs to explain." I stand, heart thudding. "Why are you looking at me like that?"

"Violet. We need to talk."

"Talk? *Talk*? If Grayson killed Wesley, he put blood on that coat and left it near the scene. He *knew* I wore the coat that night." I shake my head, attempting to dislodge the horrible truth crashing down.

Rowan blinks away his thoughts. "I detected two people with Wesley."

"Then Grayson had an accomplice." I bite hard on my lip. "Are you *sure* Leif never attacked Wesley that night?" I'm glancing between Rowan and the door but switch focus to him when he doesn't reply. "Rowan?"

"I don't know everything," he mumbles, twisting the chain round in a circle on the floor.

"What does that mean?" I half-shout. "Was he the person in the scarf?"

Rowan looks up, face strained. "Leif wouldn't kill."

"He's a shifter who'd been attacked. That triggers them. Good grief." I snatch my jacket from where I dumped it on Rowan's bed and scoop the items from the floor. "What if Wesley came across him and Leif lost his shit?"

My attempt to invade Rowan's mind fails. The familiar barrier is there, but less absolute. He's confused; I sense that much from his thoughts, even if I can't read his expression properly.

"I'm finding and talking to them both. Where's Leif?" I shove the items into my pocket.

"I don't know."

"Has he left? When you spoke in the library, you talked about Leif becoming a fugitive after doing something. Is *that* what happened?"

"No, Violet. That conversation concerns something different. Complicated. Leif wouldn't leave. He can't."

I turn away from Rowan to look out the window where the half-moon casts a weak light across the rear academy grounds, towards the woods. Has Rowan pulled me into a ruse to confuse me? Did he already know everything he showed me?

"And I don't believe Leif's capable of killing," Rowan adds.

"*Everybody* is capable," I retort, still looking through the window.

"Even you?"

My head jerks around. "Even me. Even *you*, Rowan."

Rowan stands too. "Yes. But I won't need to."

"What does that mean? Because Wesley's already dead?" I

reel against a thought that hits me. Leif's comment earlier. "Did you mind-control Leif to kill Wesley?"

"That's stupid, Violet. Grayson killed him. What motive do I have?"

I suck on my teeth and study Rowan, waiting for one expression change I might be able to recognize.

There *is* a change. Not in his manner or his mind, but in his magic. I've never noticed the dark edges, like wisps of smoke hidden in the haze.

Something familiar.

"You've played with Blackwood magic—or tried to! *You're* the one framing me with the rune? Why?"

Rowan steps towards me and looks down. "Why would I frame you if I wanted your help? Yes, I've touched Blackwood magic, but not in the way you think."

"The book." I cross my arms and back away. "Blackwood magic is in the book; that's why you wouldn't give it to me. I'm going to prove this was all you!"

"You're so damn lost in yourself that you never see the obvious, Violet. Are you really that shut down against *everything* in your world?" he snaps. "Don't you understand what just happened?"

"Yes. You tricked me." As I move towards his door, Rowan steps in front to block my way. The new shadow around him spreads. Familiar. Blackwood. "You planted the images that you *wanted* me to see into my mind. Not the truth."

"Listen to yourself! How is this logical? How can *I* trick *you*, Violet?"

"This is why I never trust anybody. Ever." Magic immediately triggers on my fingertips, but not fire this time. White sparks begin to wind around my hands, and I lift them up, palms outwards. "I suggest you let me leave, Rowan."

His face blanches. "Fuck. Violet."

"You know what this spell could do to you," I hiss at him. "And you know I can stop your heart."

"You wouldn't kill me," he says hoarsely. "Stop this. You're overreacting."

"I want a confession and for you to let me walk out of this room or I *will* stop your heart."

Rowan's jaw clenches. "You wouldn't be able to do that, Violet Blackwood."

"When will you get into your head what I'm capable of doing?" I growl.

"Do you not realize you'll never be able to hurt me?"

His voice rises and I sneer. "That's optimistic. Maybe I *am* a psychopath."

Rowan's fingers curl hard around my wrist, and I gasp out when nothing happens to him. Nothing but the lighting dancing along his arm and a pushback jolt to my heart.

"Get off me!" I yell, but his grip remains. "Rowan!"

"What did I say the first day we met, Violet?" he urges. "Like meets like. I didn't know just how alike."

Summoning everything I can, I slam a hammer of magic into Rowan's mind instead. Instantly, I reel backwards too, tearing my arm from his hold and grabbing my head, as the hammer bounces back.

"What have you done?" I yell.

"Nothing," he says softly. "Nobody *does* this."

My breath comes in faster pants, mind whirling, unfamiliar sensations rushing through my veins, pushing at my heart, my soul. My mind.

What's happening here? Nothing I've said and done in the last few minutes is *me*. I don't react like this. But now… something more grows further inside me.

Anger. Anguish. Fear.

Fury.

Whatever Rowan did punched through the barrier that I

need as much as the potion I feed myself with—the thin wall between myself and my father. I'm Dorian Blackwood's daughter. I'm everything he is and was, everything my mother didn't want me to become. She tried to change Dorian, but nobody could leash the hybrid created and trained to kill. Not totally.

Which means nobody can leash me.

Blood mist blinds me. I don't need to smell Rowan's own to give in to the frenzied desire pumping through my own. *Destroy the threat.* I'll be far away before anybody finds me.

Fear doesn't so much as flicker across Rowan's face as I lash out, nails and teeth ready to tear into him. "Stop!" Rowan catches my wrist again. "Look at me!"

As if commanded, the mist clears and in his eyes I see the worst thing imaginable.

Myself.

He tries to touch my face and I recoil. "You'll never be able to hurt me because we're witch bonded, Violet. That's the Blackwood magic I touched."

His words punch all air from my lungs. "You're lying," I shout. "This is a spell." Dragging my arm from Rowan's, I smack both hands hard in his chest. "What have you done to me?"

"Nothing! I never knew until we linked magic. Stay here. We need to talk." He drags messy hair from his pale face.

"Do you understand what you've done to me?" I shout. "That this could change me, and in a bad way? I don't want your magic."

"Nobody chooses a witch bond," he shouts back. "Do you think I'd choose you? The girl who doesn't give a shit about anybody but herself? Who doesn't care about me?"

Our synchronized breaths come as pants and everything flows through the broken dam in my mind, building and building to a crescendo nobody wants to experience.

I need to get out of here.

"You're lying," I say hoarsely one more time. "Let me out of that door. Now."

Rowan seizes my hand in both of his and I can't possibly break the grip. His eyes are wild, face flushed. "Don't go. Please. This freaked us both out and we need to talk about what to do.

"Do? Keep away from each other!"

His fingers loosen slightly but our breathing stays in rhythm. "That's the problem. I don't want to. Not because of the bond, but you. I care what happens to you, Violet; I don't want to see you get hurt."

"That *is* the bond," I snap back. "We hardly know each other. You don't care about me. Open the door."

Chapter Thirty-One

A WITCH BOND. *No.* I can't allow this to happen. *How* did this happen?

I take shuddery breaths as I walk briskly from the witches' Pendle House, headed towards the edge of campus. If I'm going to channel this out of myself, I can't do so in a public place. I'll hide like a shifter who's lost self-restraint.

I've no control over a witch bond or what this situation opened inside me—a connection with another. I'm disassociated from everything for a reason. Not only do I misunderstand people and the world, but I don't *want* to understand. I've nothing 'against' strong emotions—just, life's easier without them for me and others.

But this.

This *anger*.

Ethan and Zeke, in particular, worked with me on learning to be self-reliant. They taught me to face head on anything that threatened to release the darkness inherited from Dorian and then control my responses. Dorian himself would put me in situations that would horrify my family if they knew.

He didn't do this to hurt me but to ensure one thing: the permafrost around my magic, heart, and soul can never thaw.

Dorian once wanted the world to burn in a need for a revenge that was scorched on his soul. Eloise argued that connecting with a world outside himself extinguished *that* Dorian. Allowing himself to love her and become part of a family pulled him from the edge.

But I don't doubt he could become the old Dorian again.

Spending so much time with people while ignoring my desire for solitude has eaten away at the quiet, calm part of my mind. I'm *exhausted*.

Witch bond. The word repeats in my head, over and over. Rowan's *lying*.

And even if this bond is an undeniable truth, I'll stay away from him. Refuse to solidify what fate held for us. The physical union between bonded witches isn't inevitable, it's only the magic and soul bonds that are unavoidable.

Whatever I do now, this bond is one thing I can't control. Rowan will affect me for life; I could walk to the opposite end of the world, and he'd still be within me.

But if he has sense, he won't follow, tonight or ever.

Why didn't my vampire side *stop* this witch-only bond, like the witch side helps with the blood lust?

As I shoot through the academy's perimeter fence, I make my way towards the woods, blind to everything but unleashing the tsunami inside. If a teacher sees, they'd better not follow or things could get much, much worse. The trees close in on me, branches trailing along my bare arms and the thorned bushes scratching at my legs.

The pent-up fury unleashes, and I scream until my lungs empty, cocooned in the suffocating woods where the sky isn't visible, the trees absorbing the screaming.

Or so I thought.

Something too large to be a rabbit moves towards me.

Every muscle coils tighter, primed for attack. My magic may be exhausted, but my vampire side is ready. But what I detected moves so quickly behind me that I don't notice until somebody seizes hold, an arm around my abdomen and a hand clamped firmly across my face.

Immediately, my sharper nails rip at the fingers pressed against me, and I flail my legs as I'm lifted from the ground and dragged backwards at speed. Heavy, hissed breaths respond to my magic and physical attack, but the hold on me remains firm. Whoever holds me isn't a shifter—the solid body I'm held against isn't bulky enough, the scent all wrong. This isn't Rowan's scent, either.

Pulling my head back, I bite hard on the hand that's over my mouth, but all that happens is my assailant presses tighter. Blood zings across my tongue, and my panic grows.

I've blood in my mouth and I'm *tasting* it. How?

"Move your hand," I try to shout, but my voice is muffled. "Let me go."

I scent more blood. He stinks of it.

Desperately, I pull at the hand, using every last iota of physical and magical energy remaining after today. Finally, the magic succeeds and his grip drops, as if something dragged him backwards. I hear a thud and the sound of someone gasp for breath.

I spin around, wiping at the blood coating my lips and tongue, trembling with a primal need for more.

Grayson. "What the—" I yell, but don't finish the sentence before he's on his feet and I'm slammed backwards into a tree. Grayson's uninjured hand covers my mouth and nose, offering me some respite, and he pants as he looks down at me.

My eyes go wide. His solid muscle pushes against me, overwhelming, but that physical closeness isn't what affects my senses. There's no arousal from our unplanned intimacy

—it's the blood. I've a crazy need to lick that blood from his face.

"Listen to me," he hisses. "You can't be seen here."

"Why?" I'm muffled, confused, staring at the blood on his face. I *should* be asking 'whose blood?' but I'm beyond that.

"There's another body."

My stomach somersaults, and I pull at his hand, pulled back from the desire. Grayson killed again. "I won't scream; I don't scream."

"Uh. Yes. I just heard you."

"That's different," I say and gasp for air as his hand withdraws.

"I never expected the scream to be *you*." He drags a blood-stained hand through his hair. "I never expected Violet Blackwood to scream."

"Were you saving a damsel in distress or looking for your next hit? I know you killed Wesley!" I pinch my nose against the blood scent. "Whose blood can I smell?"

My heart stutters when he doesn't reply. *Please, no.*

"What have you done, Grayson?" I ask hoarsely. "Is this another of the bullies from school? Is *that* what you're doing? Picking them off, one by one?"

"No." He steps back. "No, no, *no*. I was coming back from…" He swipes a hand across his mouth. "A meeting."

"A meeting?" My eyes narrow. "Between your teeth and someone's jugular?"

"This isn't a joke. We need to get back to the academy," he urges, and grabs my hand.

I snatch it away. Holding hands screwed up my life once tonight. "How close to the body were you, Grayson? How were you 'conveniently' there?"

I smack a mental palm against his mind, pissed how much stronger vamps are at mental magic because all I can pick up is the mantra 'don't tell her, don't tell her' over and over.

"I tried to help again, Violet." He runs both hands through his hair this time. "But I couldn't."

"Help? Help kill?" I half-shriek and step back. "It *was* you! Who helped?"

"No." He's vehement. "But you need to leave. There's a rune on the body again."

No.

"Why? Are you framing me again?" I snarl.

"What?" I immediately slam my way into his mind; he's blocked but there's confusion edging the thoughts. "No, Violet. I didn't kill Wesley, so why and how would I frame you?"

"Then why were you seen near Wesley's body?" This time, my heart almost stops when he doesn't answer. "Rowan practices psychometry. You're imprinted on objects that were on Wesley when he was murdered. You were there and used my *coat* to frame me!"

He pinches the bridge of his nose, shaking his head, and I shove into his head again. "I don't know what hokey magic the guy used or the lies he told you." Grayson meets my eyes and the wall slips. Slightly. *Grayson genuinely doesn't understand what I mean about a coat.* "But I didn't kill Wesley."

Then what did Rowan see with the spell?

Rune. "How close did you get to the person, Grayson?"

"Close enough to hear there's no heartbeat," he says flatly. "To see the damage."

"Who?" I whisper. "Who died?"

Grayson falls quiet for a moment. "Rory. The shifter."

You'll have to pray that one of the shifters doesn't die next.

My mouth parches, all thought of blood wiped away. Until a few minutes ago, I was with Rowan. But… the other theory. "Have you seen Leif tonight?"

"He was in town earlier when I… passed through." Grayson watches me warily.

There's something missing here. Too many things out of my grasp. Out of my control.

"And recently?" Grayson shakes his head. But how long has the body been... wherever?

"We should get back to the academy before we're missed, Violet," he urges. "There's nothing we can do."

I swallow down the thickness in my throat. "You have a lot to explain to me before I believe you didn't kill Wesley. Or Rory."

"I know. And I will. But we can't be *seen* in the woods, Violet."

One death and a body with a Blackwood rune wasn't proof I murdered someone. A second time? Too big a coincidence.

Slumping to the floor, I put my face in my hands. I'm exhausted. Barely able to function mentally or physically. Who's doing this to me? And why?

Grayson crouches beside me and I shrug him off when he tries to touch my shoulder. "Violet. I promise I haven't killed anybody, and I will do everything I can to help you. To help prove you're innocent."

"Why?"

"Because despite being insignificant *to* you, I'm captivated *by* you." He laughs softly to himself. "Either you have lamia skills you're unaware of, or I must enjoy a challenge."

"Or you're insane," I mumble. "If you haven't killed anybody, let me into your mind. Show me your memories and how that blood found its way onto your face."

"I will, but please, please leave these woods before things get worse for you, Violet." He stands and holds out a hand.

A hand I accept.

I expected life at Thornwood to challenge me, but I never expected the place would *change* me. For the first time in my life, I'm losing control. Of my world. Myself. My future.

And I don't like it.

The story continues with Thornwood Academy: Dead To Me

AUTHOR NOTE

I held a competition where readers could vote for a character to be named after themselves or one they chose.

The winner of the naming competition for Violet's roommate is Holly Nicole.

And the runner-ups are minor characters who were also looking for names:
Heather Price who chose Isabella
Gina Mandel who chose Kirsten.

Congratulations to you all!

Thank you to everybody who entered

I also want to say a huge thank you to all my readers and supporters who've all had patience with me over the last few years. I appreciate every one of you and your friendship and support has helped me in some difficult times. I'm so proud to write books people love.

I always like to hear from readers so please email me at lisa@ljswallow.com if you ever want to.

All the best for 2023!